Praise for The Thinking Tomato

Jim Martin has been my leader, my colleague, my mentor, and my friend for many years. Jim has always appreciated the value of storytelling as a lever for organizational change and personal growth. His book, *The Thinking Tomato*, is no exception. Set in a corporate environment and told through the eyes of a young engineer, Jerry Artson, this book chronicles Jerry's personal journey as he becomes acquainted with Mother Nature and what she has to teach. Whether it's the importance of true observation, or the relationship between the flower and the bee, Jerry slowly realizes that the secret to happiness lies all around him if he'll just take the time to notice. Indeed, the road to personal mastery may very well wind its way through a vegetable garden.

Mike Harvey, Change Facilitator, The Dow Chemical Co.

It is my pleasure to write this review for Jim Martin's innovative book *The Thinking Tomato*. As a teacher of management classes for the last two decades , I appreciate Jim's ability to distill key management concepts in a simple yet creative way. Jerry is the story's protagonist and as he learns gardening lessons from Mary, the organizational and self management teachings unfold. Consistent with the books theme and innovative insights, Jim refers to these concepts as "organizational gardening" and "self cultivation". By exploring the secrets of the Thinking Tomato and the Seven P's, it became clear that successful organizational and self management requires the same care, attention and planning as gardening. I enjoyed Jerry's adventure and gained knowledge about gardening, myself and new insights into how to lead others.

Janice Townsend, Professor of Child Development,
Los Medanos College, Pittsburg, Ca

Author Jim Martin's new management text is a new breed of business book. Innovative and creative, it takes a humanistic approach to tricky management issues. The *Thinking Tomato* goes beyond the usual formula management guides by creating a world populated with sympathetic characters with human scale issues and challenges to convey the major themes and messages. This gentle book teaches fundamental life lessons and insightful management theory through a natural progression of events in the characters' lives rather than through dry case book studies. For the newly promoted manager to the senior executive with decades of experience, there is much to be learned from this compelling and easy-to-read book.

Kathy Moore, Rossland, BC, Canada

For me reading "The Thinking Tomato" was like cleaning my glasses and seeing how dirt and smudges on the lenses were distorting my actions, attitudes, and sense of contentment. I realized that a lot of the glare, stress, and ugliness I saw in life were actually illusions that I have control over. Through the use of gardening as a metaphor the book illustrates the difference between observation and interpretation and how significant that is in our attitudes toward people, our jobs, our lives, and our happiness. We can control things that upset or anger us by either changing the situations or by changing how we see them. Or we can let those things control us by feeling helpless and victimized. In gardening it's easy to become obsessed with controlling weeds and insects and forget to appreciate the beauty of the life we're trying to nurture and cultivate. Sitting quietly and observing the plants and birds in a garden gives me a sense of peace and serenity and "The Thinking Tomato" does the same.

Chuck Higashi, San Francisco, Ca.

"The Thinking Tomato" artfully weaves important lessons about *cultivating* and motivating oneself and one's organization into a memorable story with characters you get to admire and love. Motivating leaders with high EQ are not easy to find in organizations. "The Thinking Tomato" will get you to *think* about how to motivate yourself and how to motivate others to take risks and excel unleashing the energy within organizations.

Kiran Kamath, Dean of Career Technical Education,
Los Medanos College, Pittsburg, Ca.

I have read Jim Martin's book, *The Thinking Tomato*; and even gave it to my son who works at Intel. I found the book very insightful and feel it should be required reading for all management in any business. It is both fun to read and motivational.
I highly recommend it.

Steven I Subotnick, DPM, DC
Founder and Past President of the American Academy of Podiatric Sports Medicine.
Past Clinical Professor Biomechanics and Foot and Ankle Surgery
Private Practice-San Leandro, Ca.

The Thinking Tomato
& the Seven P's

A Motivational Story About

Organizational Gardening

and Self-Cultivation

By: Jim Martin

Breezeway Books

This material is designed to provide general information about the subject matter covered. Use is granted with the understanding that the publisher and author are not engaged in rendering legal, financial or psychological advice. If expert assistance is required in these areas, the services of a competent professional should be sought.

The purpose of this information is to educate and entertain. The author and publisher shall have neither liability nor responsibility to any person or entity with respect to any loss or damage caused, or alleged to be caused, directly or indirectly, by the information contained here.

ISBN: 978-1-62550-458-6 (PB)

Dedication

This book is dedicated to my wife, Claire, and daughter, Anastasie. May they always know that life is what you make it to be.

Acknowledgements

My thanks to the following people and organizations:

To Gail Heidenhain of Delphin International for exposing me to the principles of *Accelerated Learning* which makes learning fun and effective.

To the Ken Blanchard Companies for the opportunity to facilitate the course *Situational Self Leadership* where I learned a tremendous amount about how to influence myself and others.

To the FranklinCovey company for the opportunity to facilitate the course, *The Seven Habits of Highly Effective People.*

To the San Francisco Bay Area Society of Organizational Learning for the opportunity to participate in ongoing dialogue sessions on Organizational Learning.

To Kathy Moore for the multitude of recommendations she provided for improving my book and to the following people who also provided feedback:

Carmen Thieson, Margaret McGillivray, Mike Harvey, Thomas Evans, Mike Cavitt, Gregory McGrath, Antonia McKinney, Judy Deverill, Raymon Yates, John Garcia, Janice Townsend, Kiran Kamath, Steve Subotnick, Elizabeth Doty, Jim McCaughan, Tom Brewer, Dennis Smith, Gail Pearson, Hope Scurran, Mike Martin, Gary Demarest, Susan Fowler, John Muraglia, Faye McCaughan, George Russo.

Table of Contents

Prologue

A conversation takes place in the employee parking lot about quitting time on a Friday at Microprojects, Inc., a hi-tech firm in Santa Clara County, California.

Jerry: Can you believe what just happened? I've about had it!

Gene: What's wrong now, Jer? You had a meeting with Mad Man Mills?

Jerry: How'd you ever guess? He leaves me a message this morning saying he wants to see me at 1:00. I'm there on time, but he shows up a half hour late, says he just got out of a meeting with Blackburn. Didn't apologize or anything!

Gene: Typical Mills. So what was the meeting about?

Jerry: Oh, he wanted me to redo some numbers on one of the projects. Evidently the calculations I gave him weren't to the "big man's" liking. Mills probably promised him something ridiculous, and now I have to make it work. He's the only person I know who expects you to put ten pounds of stuff into a two-pound bag. It's just getting to be too much.

Gene: What do you make of our new honcho, Blackburn? I heard he worked his way through college at a meat market. That's where he became so good at carving off the fat. Now they've sent him out here to practice on us.

Jerry: I wouldn't doubt it at all. Somebody mentioned that his nickname is "The Carver." Wonder if he realizes people call him that? Did you hear that Jeff Winston got canned yesterday? Rita said she saw him loading all of his stuff into his car.

Gene: No, I hadn't heard. Knowing Jeff, he was probably stealing the stuff; no big loss there. Anyway, that's the fifth one this month!

Jerry: Dropping like flies! Wonder who is next?

Gene: Don't know; maybe you. Not me, though; the place would collapse if I left; I mean who'd take care of the office grapevine?

Jerry: Good point. But for me it's a sobering thought. Well, I've been meaning to dust off my resume. It's such a shame, though. This company used to be a good place to work.

Gene: When was that? I don't remember it ever being that great. Isn't it funny how the "good old days" are the good old days except *during* the good old days?

Jerry: What do you mean?

Gene: Think about it, Jer. It's too simple to explain. Hey, what you got going this weekend?

Jerry: I've been thinking about planting another vegetable garden, something to get my mind off this place.

Gene: A garden, huh? Like that weed patch you planted last year? Least you proved beyond any shadow of a doubt that you can't grow plants without water. What a waste of time and energy, though. I'm going to continue getting my vegetables at a reliable place: the market. Well, call me if you'd like to grab a beer.

Jerry: You call that stuff they sell at the supermarket *vegetables?* Last time I bought tomatoes, they tasted more like watermelon minus the sweet taste. Anyway, I'm going to give it a try. Catch you later, Gene.

Chapter One

Down in the Doldrums

Jerry Artson had just turned thirty-two; he was tall and dark with outdoorsy, rugged good looks, a degree in electrical engineering from a prestigious West Coast school, and a well-paying position with a Silicon Valley firm, Microprojects, Inc. He should have felt like he was on top of the world. Instead, he felt like the world was sitting on top of him. Six months ago he had broken up with a girl he had been dating for four years. She had started seeing someone else. She said it was because Jerry was so negative about everything, particularly work. Now she was engaged to the guy. It was just one more thing in a series of mishaps in his life. To be honest, he *was* negative about his job and life in general, but who wouldn't be?

He had been working at Microprojects for ten years, but it seemed like it had all been wasted time. What a disappointment; thirty-two years old and his life was going nowhere! Go to work, look at the clock, go home, spend his non-working time thinking about how much he disliked work, and then start the cycle again. And his distaste for his work life seemed to spill over into the weekends, vacation, and all facets of his personal life. He was a mess.

It was not so much that he disliked what he was doing; as a project manager for the design and development of multicomputer system installations, he had worked on some very challenging projects, and he was able to interact with a lot of interesting people. The real problem was management. Ever since Joe Blackburn had taken over as division manager a year ago, things had gone downhill. Perhaps it was because of the downsizing and reengineering that had taken place with many firms in the Bay Area recently. No one trusted management anymore. And Joe and his faithful middle-level managers didn't trust any of the workers either; at least it appeared that way. Otherwise why did *they* have to make all the decisions? They talked about something they called *empowerment*, but command and control was alive and well at Microprojects, that was for sure! As usual, talk was cheap.

This was the start of the weekend. He felt he should at least try not to let his miserable work life continue to spoil his personal life. Jerry was on his way to the nursery to buy some plants. He had decided to plant a garden. Maybe this would get his mind off work. He was going to The Green Patch Nursery, and Mary Green, the owner, was a longtime friend of Jerry's mother.

Jerry guessed Mary was somewhere in her fifties because she was about the same age as his mother, but you couldn't tell by looking at her. She was in great physical shape. Long hair down past her waist, fine features, and piercing, almost hypnotic, aqua-green eyes, gave her an ageless kind of beauty. If she hadn't been a friend of his mother's, he would never have guessed her age. Ten years ago Mary's husband, John, had died in an airplane accident along with their son, Benjamin. John, a private pilot, had taken Benjamin for a flight over the Sierras and an aerial view of Yosemite Valley when a mechanical problem with their plane caused it to stall. Grief-stricken but strong-minded Mary decided it was time to act upon the *dream* she had had all her life, so she had taken the insurance money and bought a nursery. Jerry's mom had sketched the outcome of her life, but Jerry didn't know any more of the details.

Now, Mary seemed to have the perfect job. Despite her losses in the past, she was always upbeat and engrossed in her work, and it was contagious. Jerry always felt better when he was around Mary. Her last name was "Green" and, coincidence or not, she sure did have a green thumb. She could make anything grow. Her yard was full of the most beautiful plants he had ever seen. The Green Patch Nursery was the most successful nursery in the area. All the employees were as upbeat as Mary. As he drove to the nursery, he was thinking maybe he should have studied horticulture or botany instead of electrical engineering.

Jerry walked into the nursery and found Mary on her knees at the back of the store with her hands buried in soil. Several empty pots sat by her side, and a stack of bare-root rose plants was piled in front. Even though Mary was the owner, most of the time she was indistinguishable from her employees.

"Hello, Mary," Jerry called as he walked over to her. "Why don't you try and get some of that dirt in the pots?" he asked jokingly. Mary jumped slightly.

"Oh, hi, Jerry. What a nice surprise!" Mary said with a broad smile as she looked up from her work. "Boy, I haven't seen you in a long time. How have you been, and how is your mom doing?"

Jerry's mother and Mary had been roommates for a while when they were in college and had maintained contact over the years. His parents had lived in Atlanta, but after Jerry's father passed away two years earlier, his mother had moved in with one of Jerry's two brothers and his family in Florida.

"She's doing great," Jerry said. "She and two of her friends are on a six-week cruise in the Caribbean. They left last week. Since dad past away, she's only stayed around the house. I think she was starting to drive my brother crazy. It will be good for both of them if she gets away for a bit. Maybe this cruise is just what she needs. It's not easy to lose someone you have been with for many years, but you of all people should know that," he trailed off, slightly embarrassed.

"Yes, how well I do, Jerry. Well tell her I said hello when you talk to her again. Have her give me a call so I can hear about her trip. Is this a social visit or are you looking for some plants?"

"I'm here for both, Mary. It's always a pleasure to see you, but I'm really interested in starting a garden, and I need some help. The garden I planted last year was a catastrophe. I never have any luck with growing plants. My thumb definitely isn't green, and, as of late, my bad luck with plants has been spilling over into my work. Everything I touch seems to be turning brown," he moaned.

Mary's smile faded. "Is there something wrong at work, Jerry?"

"Yes. In fact, I'm to the point where I can't stand the place. But I don't want to burden you with my problems."

Mary paused for a moment and then said, "But Jerry, I thought you enjoyed what you do. You always said that your life's dream was to be an electrical engineer. You used to love your job. What's happened?"

"It's not so much what I do, but the new management. Ever since that new guy, Joe Blackburn, took over as division manager, it's been different. I just don't have the chance to be myself. I feel like I'm in a prison at work. Joe and his tight circle of favorites make all the decisions. Us 'peons' just do what we're told. I'm getting so fed up with it I feel like quitting!"

Mary finished placing a plant into a pot and covered it with soil. She looked up at Jerry with a quizzical expression and asked mildly, "So, Jerry, you don't seem very happy. What are you planning to do about it?"

Jerry whined, "Do? What can I do? I'll just continue getting my paychecks and hope we get another manager eventually. Some people are lucky and some are not, but how can I possibly do anything about it? Microprojects has changed for the worse. Most of the people like me working there just try to do their jobs and hope they don't receive a 'pink slip' surprise one day. Heck, last month, they let five more people go! You sure don't want to make any waves or you might be next. Keep your mouth shut, do your job, and keep a low profile. That's my motto."

Mary looked seriously at Jerry and said, "Doesn't sound like a great situation."

Jerry responded, "No, it sure isn't. But more and more that seems to be the norm today. At least that's what some of my friends who work at other companies in The Valley confirm. Maybe it's a sign of the times," he said, shaking his head. Then he looked around and said, "But it doesn't seem to be the norm here. How come you and all the people working here are so full of life and seem to enjoy your work so much? Maybe it's the difference between horticulture and engineering. Some jobs are just more fun."

"I thought you said you liked your work but management was the problem," said Mary.

Jerry thought for a moment and said, "Yeah, well, that's true. It's management's actions that cause me to not like what I do because at one time I did like my job, in pre-Blackburn days! He has changed things so much in the last year. The bottom line has always ruled, but now it's ruling with an iron fist." He thought for a moment and said, "So if management is the problem, what type of management do you have here that allows your employees to be so turned on by their jobs? After all, you're the boss."

Mary was silent for a moment as she looked out over the rosebushes, and then she said, "I guess we've learned from the plants, Jerry. This is after all a nursery."

"From the plants?" he asked with a confused look.

"Yes, we treat our employees like we treat the plants," Mary stated with a smile.

"You mean you water them?" Jerry asked jokingly.

"Not exactly, Jerry," Mary laughed. "But I've found that good leaders should first be good gardeners, not only because this is a nursery. If you create an environment in which plants can thrive, they probably will. The same holds true for people. Create the right environment and things will take care of themselves. Ignore it and who knows where it will go? Most of the time, downhill, just like when you ignored your garden last year. Here we call the whole process *organizational gardening.*"

"That's very interesting. Can you tell me what that environment is and what organizational gardening is?" Jerry asked, perking up a little.

Mary smiled and said, "I would love to talk to you about it, Jerry, but I don't have time to even start describing it right now. Although it's simple and very basic in some ways, in other ways it's rather complicated. Tell you what; you said you were looking for some plants to grow. There's no better way to learn about organizational gardening. You remember I said leaders should first be good gardeners?"

"But I didn't say anything about being a leader. I'm just curious. I'll send Blackburn over if you want to teach leadership skills. Obviously *he* needs the training," Jerry said.

"And I'm sure he'll run right over here if you tell him he needs to be a gardener," Mary laughed.

"Probably not," Jerry smirked. "Besides, I've never even met the guy!"

"Well, you might not be interested in being a leader," Mary said, "but you're probably interested in leading yourself, and the same thing applies with regard to creating an environment. Did you ever work for someone who couldn't lead himself or herself, Jerry?"

"You bet. I'm working for one now, Andy Mills. He's a total idiot. I don't see how he finds his way to work in the morning."

Mary realized it was time to change the subject. "Hmm . . . maybe we can discuss your boss some other time. You mentioned you're looking for some plants. What kind?" she asked.

"I'd like something that is easy to grow and requires little care. Cactus would be about my speed," Jerry said jokingly.

"Well, with gardening, as with most things, you get out of it as much as you put into it. Let's narrow it down. Are you looking for flowers or vegetables or something else?"

"Vegetables, I think. Might as well be able to use what I plant. Something like tomatoes, that type of plant."

"An excellent choice, Jerry. Growing tomatoes can be very educational. In fact, the whole history of the tomato is very interesting. The tomato plant, or *Lycopersicon esculentum,* as it is technically known, is of the nightshade family and is related to the potato and eggplant. Although cultivated in Mexico and Peru for centuries before the European conquest, the tomato is one of the newest plants to be used on a large scale for human food. When the Spanish explorers brought back seed from South America, the plant was grown merely as an ornament; it was known as the *love apple*. Though the fruit was described as a salad ingredient before 1600, it was commonly regarded as poisonous, and only within the last century has it become recognized as a valuable food. Indeed, all parts of the plant but the fruit are toxic to humans. It was reintroduced to the United States as a food plant in the 1800s and now ranks third among our vegetable crops. Today it's known that the tomato is one of the most healthful vegetables there is. So how can something so healthful be thought to be poisonous? There's a lesson in this, Jerry, a very powerful message about how accurately we see the world, about our mental models. So tomatoes are a good choice. Let's throw in some celery, beans, cucumbers, lettuce, and zucchini to round out your garden. You'll be able to make a real nice salad in a few months. How's that sound?"

"Great, Mary," Jerry responded, a little overwhelmed. "You have any instructions on what I should do? I don't want to make the same mistakes I made the last time I tried to grow a garden."

"Well, a little water might help," she said, laughing. "I'll give you a book on gardening, but seriously, most of it is common sense. Remember, if you create the right environment, your plants will do just fine. After they have started growing and you've learned something significant, particularly something about yourself, come back and we can discuss it and I can tell you more about organizational gardening. Of course, if you have any problems, you can call me anytime."

"Uh, OK," Jerry said, nodding his head with a confused look. "I'll, uh . . . I'll give it a try."

Jerry, with tomato plants and other vegetables neatly boxed, left the nursery feeling a little at odds. Seeing Mary was always like a breath of fresh air. She had a certain charisma that gave one the feeling that she was well grounded and stable. At least his conversation with her had taken his mind off his job for a while. He was looking forward to planting a garden. And he was very intrigued by what she had said about treating people the way she treated her plants. But he was wondering what she meant when she said that the story of the tomato plant was a very powerful lesson about how accurately we see the world. What lesson was that? And what significant lessons about himself was he supposed to learn by growing vegetables? It didn't make a lot of sense to him.

Chapter Two

Planting the Garden

When Jerry arrived home, he placed his tomatoes and other plants in the shade, grabbed a cold drink from the refrigerator, and sat down to read about gardening. He opened the book to the section on growing tomatoes and read:

> **Tomatoes are easy to grow and provide one of the greatest rewards in home gardening. They should be planted in the spring when there is no danger of frost. Plant them in direct sunlight in a rich soil mix that drains well. Plants do best when two or more are planted close to each other. This allows for the cross pollination of the flowers. Tomato plants are very prone to caterpillars that can totally destroy a tomato plant in a few days. Sprinkle the plant with an approved vegetable insecticide after flowers appear on the plant, or if you prefer, inspect the plant daily and remove the caterpillars. Be aware; they are very difficult to see because their color and form blend in well with the plant.**

Jerry went on to read about the other plants. When he finished, he gathered his garden tools and set about preparing a six-by-ten-foot area in his back yard. The gardening book had mentioned the importance of using a solution of vitamin B-1 to help the plants adjust and get through the shock of being transplanted, but he had neglected to get any when he was at the nursery. Also, he knew the adobe earth was very hard so he needed some soil conditioner, too. Not wanting to start out wrong, he decided to return to the nursery and pick up a bottle. When he arrived he looked around for Mary, but she was nowhere to be found. He stopped one of the employees and asked her if she knew where Mary was. The employee had *Jennifer* on her name tag. What looked like an apple or a tomato was sewn on the other side of her shirt. Jennifer offered to help him since Mary would not be back for a couple of hours.

"I need to pick up some vitamin B-1 and soil conditioner. I was here earlier, and Mary helped me choose some plants to start a vegetable garden, but I forgot the B-1 and conditioner."

Jennifer smiled and said, "The B-I is right over here." She walked over to a shelf and grabbed a quart bottle. "This should be enough unless you are planning to plant a large garden. Bags of soil conditioner are on aisle nine. How big is your garden?"

"About six by ten feet", Jerry replied.

"Then, six bags should do fine. If you don't use it all, you can return the unused bags", Jennifer said. "Anything else you need?"

"No, I don't think so," Jerry responded, hesitating a bit. "Although I am curious about what that apple-looking thing is on your shirt? I've seen it on other employees here, and Mary had one on her shirt too."

"It's not supposed to represent an apple," Jennifer said, laughing. "It's supposed to be a tomato, a *thinking* tomato. It's part of our nursery philosophy of organizational gardening."

"A thinking tomato . . . You've gotta be kidding! Mary mentioned something about organizational gardening when I talked to her earlier, but she didn't say anything about *thinking* tomatoes. She said it was about creating the right environment for plants to grow and for people to grow."

"Exactly," Jennifer said, nodding her head. "That's what it's about."

"But what does it have to do with a *thinking* tomato?" Jerry asked, looking a little confused.

"Well, creating the right environment consists of a lot of factors, like proper resources, open communication, and proper training, just to name a few, but probably the most important is the ability to take control and think for yourself, to be proactive, master of your own destiny, those types of things," Jennifer said. "Of course, the 'thinking tomato' is only a metaphor. You can't teach a tomato how to think, but people can be taught."

"But don't most people already know how? How can one become an adult and not know how to think?" Jerry said, looking even more confused.

"Unfortunately not," Jennifer said, frowning slightly. "Look around at the people you encounter every day. Are they in charge or are they complaining about their state, blaming the government, their employers, their spouses, their parents, or whomever or whatever?"

Jerry turned a little red and looked down at his feet, embarrassed that she might well have been referring to him. "I guess you're right. That's about all that goes on at work nowadays. But a lot of it seems justified. I mean, what with all the stuff management has been doing to us lately, what's so wrong with complaining? It lets off steam."

"Nothing" Jennifer said, smiling. "Particularly if you don't want anything to change. You see, we have only three choices, and only two of them are any good. Change the situation or change the way we see it or a combination of the two."

"That's only two. What's the third?" Jerry asked.

"The third choice is never a good option," she responded. "But it is the one that too many people, I might say most people, choose too often: play the victim. Complain about it. Blame whatever is the problem on someone else. Short term, it often appears to be the right route to take because it relieves the individual of any responsibility, any need to take action. But long term, it is a pitfall that can create tremendous frustration."

"But lots of situations are very difficult or even impossible to change," Jerry whined, feeling his ego was getting a little bruised.

"No one ever said that everything would be easy," Jennifer said. "But working here with Mary and the others, I've learned I can make positive major changes in my life, stuff that before I believed was impossible."

"Hmmm," said Jerry as he thought about what she had said. "What you say is very intriguing. Maybe I can learn some more about it. Mary has given me some homework already. She asked me to see what significant things I can learn as I grow my garden. Which reminds me, I had better get back to planting the vegetables before they die. It's been a pleasure talking to you, Jennifer. Tell Mary I'm sorry I missed her."

"Will do," Jennifer said. "Good luck with your garden."

Jerry drove home contemplating the conversation he had just had with Jennifer. *I'll need to think some more about what she said,* he thought. It all sounds fine, but real life doesn't work like that. Most things we don't have control over. Was Jennifer being a little idealistic and unrealistic or maybe just naïve? She looks like a fairly young woman who has everything going for her. What could she possibly know about difficult challenges?

After arriving home, Jerry began preparing the soil. With a spade in hand, he turned over the soil to create a six by ten foot plot. The earth was very hard and dry, and it was very strenuous work. He began to sweat profusely. As he turned over the clods of soil he ran into several large stones and rocks which he tossed aside. After creating the approximate plot he went back and broke up the large clods with a hoe. Next, he added the bags of soil conditioner and blended them in with a shovel. Once the conditioner was in and the soil had a fine, smooth consistency, he fashioned several furrows in the plot so he could add the plants. Carefully, he dug a small hole for each seedling adding water and B-1 as directed, then planting each in a hole and gently covering it with soil. It took over three hours to complete and he was tired, sweaty, dirty, and achy when he finished. It was a lot of work but he felt something he hadn't felt in a long time; he felt happy and he hadn't thought about his job even once. The work tilling and preparing the soil gave him a keen appetite. He went inside and prepared a spaghetti dinner. To celebrate 'the garden' he opened a nice Cabernet. Sipping the wine after the meal, he sat back feeling that somehow changes in his life might be imminent. He thought about what Mary had asked him to do, and he tried to think what he had learned while planting his garden, but could come up with nothing except that hard work relaxes the mind and you should make a list of what you need before starting a project. That way you weren't driving back and forth to the store like some idiot. Then, again, the trip back had probably been worth it. His conversation with Jennifer had given him more ideas to mull over.

Chapter Three

Meeting with Andy Mills

*M*onday morning came around much too quickly. Jerry's euphoria over the weekend's activities came to an abrupt halt when the alarm went off and he realized it was Monday morning. Getting up was no fun, particularly when it meant starting another week at Microprojects. Where did the weekend go, anyway? Jerry had a meeting scheduled with his boss, Andy Mills, first thing Monday and another one later in the week. Andy, part of Joe Blackburn's close circle of managers, was responsible for the department in which Jerry worked. When the company had downsized and consolidated some of the departments, Andy had become his new boss. He was typical of many of the people who had been promoted to leadership positions from the technical ranks; although his technical and project-management skills were exemplary, his ability to develop, motivate, and lead people was poor. Microprojects had no program for training their new managers and supervisors in how to deal with people. For this reason, and because of Andy's somewhat cocky personality, Jerry didn't particularly care for him. It seemed he was always trying to look good at the expense of the people who worked for him.

Jerry was five minutes early for the meeting. Andy's door was cracked open. Jerry knocked on the door. Andy was on the phone but waved Jerry in. Jerry sat in front of Andy's desk. The chair was somewhat uncomfortable and a little low.

Andy hung up the phone and said, "Good morning, Jerry. How was the weekend?"

"Not bad, Andy. I've started a garden in my back yard and . . ."

Andy interrupted him. "Great, great . . . do you have the status report on the McCabe project?"

Guess he doesn't care about gardening, Jerry thought. The McCabe project was one of the more interesting projects Jerry had worked on. It was his responsibility to manage the contract and, along with two other engineers, do the design, purchasing, and installation of a new computer control system at McCabe. The other two engineers were very competent. Jerry had done a similar project two years before. He had learned a lot from that work and knew exactly what to do to avoid the same mistakes this time. But Andy wanted to conduct these weekly reviews anyway. If this meeting was anything like the previous ones, Andy would make a lot of suggestions about things he knew nothing about, but Jerry knew they were more than suggestions; they were demands. Jerry usually left these meetings dejected and feeling even lower than when he pried himself out of bed in the morning.

Jerry started out, "The project is on schedule. Design is ninety percent complete, and the purchasing is coming along well . . ."

"Are you purchasing the consoles from Anderson Supplies?" Andy interrupted.

"No, we decided to go with Warren Brothers. Although they were slightly more expensive, we feel their product's quality compensates for the extra expense. It's what I would want if I owned McCabe."

"But you don't," Andy shot back. "The extra cost is a waste of money. And besides, Joe likes Anderson Supplies. He and Jack Anderson are golf buddies."

Jerry realized it was futile to argue. Andy had that "tone" that meant "Do it," so he moaned, "OK, whatever you think," and let the matter drop.

The meeting continued in the same tone. Andy talked to Jerry like he was a brand-new project manager who had never handled a contract of this type, not the seasoned project manager he actually was. Jerry just sat there and got angrier and more depressed the longer Andy talked; best to say nothing. Now he would have to go back and tell the other engineers on the project things he knew were wrong. Although Jerry never said so, they knew Andy made the decisions. They seemed to feel sorry for Jerry. Usually, after one of these meetings, the whole group sat around and bashed Andy and the rest of management.

Jerry had another meeting scheduled with Andy on Thursday. This meeting was to discuss an upcoming project to install a special computer system at Latchen, Inc. Although this project was considerably smaller than the McCabe project, Jerry had never worked with this computer system before. Despite his general mood and lack of satisfaction with Microprojects, he was excited about working on something new and learning some new skills.

In the evenings Jerry worked in his garden. He could swear the plants had already started to grow. He wanted to do something to help them grow faster; maybe more fertilizer or water. He looked intently at the garden but still couldn't figure out what Mary thought he could learn about *organizational* gardening. Jerry guessed the only thing he could do was be patient, and patience was not part of his nature.

On Thursday morning, Jerry showed up at his 10:00 meeting with Andy five minutes early. Andy was nowhere to be seen, although his office was open. Jerry walked in and sat down. As he looked around Andy's office, he noticed a lot of degrees and certificates on the walls. Everything was so neat; there wasn't a paper anywhere. He wondered if this guy ever did any real work. Andy had a huge oak desk, large paintings on the wall, and a framed picture of himself, Microprojects' CEO Jim Crabtree, and Joe Blackburn on his desk. *Must be something to be part of the "big team",* Jerry sarcastically thought.

At 10:20, Andy finally walked in, obviously in a hurry. "Hello, Jerry. How's it going? What's up?"

Perplexed, Jerry responded, "We had a meeting at 10 to discuss the Latchen project."

"The Latchen project? Oh, sorry. I must have forgotten. I have my mind on some real important things, and I have a meeting with Joe at 10:30, so we'll need to make it quick. What do you need to know?"

Uh, I'm not sure what to do. I'm excited about this project, but it is a system I haven't worked with before. I think I need some help."

"Nonsense, Jerry. This is a small project compared to the ones you've had before. And besides, Latchen is not one of our key customers."

Jerry thought, *Guess their manager doesn't play golf with Joe Blackburn*, but he said, "But they may be someday." *And certainly will never be if we botch this one,* he thought to himself.

"Whatever, but I'm sure you can figure it out. Why else do you think we pay you the big bucks?" Andy laughed. "Sorry, but I need to get to Joe's meeting. I don't want to be late. You know how Joe is about people who aren't prompt."

"But . . ." Jerry mumbled, "I . . ." as Andy rushed out of the room looking at his watch as if it had the answer to some ancient puzzle written on its face.

Jerry closed his office door and spent the rest of the afternoon staring at the screensaver on his monitor and feeling sorry for himself. He hadn't thought that things could get any worse, but the meeting with Andy proved they could. Andy's behavior was so inconsistent! When Jerry needed help, Mills just blew him off, and when he didn't need it, Mills was helping in ways that were no help at all.

Friday, Jerry decided to call in sick, although he was just depressed and disgusted with work. He had had a fitful night's sleep, dozing off for no more than thirty or forty minutes at a time and then lying awake for hours in between, dredging up all of the terrible events in his life: his breakup with his girlfriend, the loss of his father, and how much he hated work. He vaguely recalled dreaming about a fistfight with Andy Mills in the middle of the corporate cafeteria. It all started when Mills told Jerry to take back his chicken sandwich and get a hamburger. Jerry threw his lunch at Mills, and a fight started. He couldn't remember who won. After calling work at 7:30, he finally dropped off into a deep sleep, waking at 11:00.

The rest of the day he wandered around the yard, checking out his garden. Gradually he started to feel better as he focused on what he needed to do. When he planted the tomatoes, evidently he had forgotten to sufficiently water one of them because it had wilted and appeared to be dying. One thing he had discovered: if you don't water your plants, they will die; if you are not kind to your employees, they may call in ill when they aren't sick at all. Maybe this was what Mary was talking about. He got the hose and gave all the plants a good soaking. He decided he would stop by and see Mary the coming weekend and share his discovery with her.

Chapter Four

Observation and Interpretation

*J*erry woke early Saturday, feeling refreshed. The week was behind him like a bad case of the flu. After a hearty breakfast, he checked out his vegetable garden. Yes, some of the plants were beginning to grow. It looked like a flower was beginning to form on one of the tomato plants. Another week or two and the plants would be taking off. Just to be safe, he gave them another soaking with the hose.

Jerry decided to go see Mary early. He recalled that the nursery could be a zoo on Saturdays, so he wanted to have time to talk to her before it got too busy. As Jerry walked into The Green Patch, he ran into Jennifer.

"Morning, Jerry. How's it going?"

"OK, Jennifer. Is Mary around?"

"She's in the back by the rose bushes. How's your garden doing?"

"I've lost only one plant so far. I wanted to talk to Mary about what I've learned."

"Great, Jerry. I'm sure she'll be interested. If I can be of any help, let me know." She watched him pick his way to the back as he walked carefully through the rows of plants.

As Jerry walked to the back of the nursery he passed several employees. All of them smiled at him and said hello. Their friendliness gave him a lift. His mood was getting better and better. He noticed all of them had the "smiling tomato" patch on their shirts.

Jerry found Mary in the midst of a field of potted roses. The colors were beautiful, and the blossoms infused the air with a pleasant, sweet aroma. She was busy cutting dead blossoms from

21

the plants and seemed to be so engrossed in her work that she didn't notice Jerry as he walked up.

"Hey, Mary. You sure picked a nice place to work."

Surprised, Mary jumped slightly. "Oh, Jerry! I didn't hear you walk up. Sorry; what did you say?"

"I said you picked a nice place to work. One thing I've never figured out, though, is why you are out here. It seems like the owner/manager should be inside the office 'managing' rather than out here doing manual labor."

"I think you answered your own question, Jerry. I picked a nice place to work. This is what I like to do, so this is what I do. You'll probably find that if you talk to any of the other nursery associates, the same applies. They are doing what they like to do, too. I don't particularly like all of the paperwork in the office, though sometimes I have to do it, but we have associates here who enjoy that type of work. So they do what they like, and I do what I like. Shouldn't we?"

"Uh, you should, I guess, but it doesn't convey much of a boss image and, besides, you're the owner."

"Ownership is just a state of mind," Mary responded. "I'm not interested in a 'boss image,' Jerry. Image is not part of organizational gardening, at least not in that sense. Doing what one likes, as long as it is aligned with the organization's goals, is very much a part of organizational gardening, and I have chosen to do what I enjoy."

"So everyone who works here likes what they do?" Jerry responded in a slightly skeptical tone.

"Yes, Jerry, I would say so. Not every minute of every day, but most of the time. We have had employees who couldn't seem to find something here they enjoyed, but they eventually decided to leave. I believe all the people working here feel that they're empowered, and part of empowerment is choosing personal goals that fit with the organization's goals."

"Makes sense to me," Jerry said thoughtfully as he gazed off toward the horizon.

"How did it go at work last week, Jerry?"

"Not very well," Jerry said morosely as his demeanor dove from thoughtful introspection to dejection. "My boss, Andy

Mills, is so inconsistent. The management school he attended must have taught him that you feed employees when they are full and starve them when they're hungry. At least, that's the way he treats me!"

Mary gazed at him for a few moments and then asked, "And how about your garden? How is it doing?"

Jerry brightened a little and said, "Oh, fairly well. I think I may have learned something that relates to your organizational gardening," he said, and then he described what he had seen.

"So my conclusion is that water is like love or kindnesses in the sense that when we give the plants water they grow, and when management helps their employees, they grow too," Jerry said, beaming.

"Partially true," Mary said. "But you may be a little premature in your assessment."

"How so?" Jerry asked disappointedly.

Mary looked at Jerry for a few moments as if trying to decide how to answer him. Jerry was starting to feel uncomfortable when finally she said, "Tell you what, come with me to my office and I'll share something that may help you better understand."

Jerry followed Mary to her office in the back of the nursery. The room was very neat. There was a small desk on one side, but most of the space was taken up by a couple of ample sofas, a coffee table, and three large, comfortable-looking stuffed leather chairs. Various pictures of exotic flowering plants adorned the walls. In one corner, where it could be easily seen from the sofas and chairs, was a large flip chart. Mary asked Jerry to have a seat, and then she walked to the chart.

"Watch what I do, Jerry," Mary said. To his surprise, she made a bunch of odd moves and mimicked several different facial expressions. She stomped her foot, snapped her fingers, shook her head back and forth, looked down at the floor, then at the ceiling, frowned, squinted her eyes, and made an expression with her mouth that looked like she was totally disgusted. All of this took no more than thirty seconds or so, after which she walked over to the flip chart, picked up a green marker and a red marker, and asked, "Now, what did you *see*, Jerry?"

Jerry was still taken aback by Mary's behavior, but he thought for a moment and said, "You were obviously angry about something."

Mary wrote *angry* with the red marker and asked, "What else did you *see?*"

Disappointed that he hadn't hit on the answer at first, he thought for a moment and said, "You were frustrated."

Mary wrote *frustrated* on the chart in red and asked again, "What else?"

"You were confused."

She wrote *confused* in red and asked, "What else?"

"You had forgotten something and were trying to remember it," Jerry responded, thinking this time he had certainly hit on the right answer.

Mary again wrote in red *forgot something.* "What else?" she asked as she looked at him quizzically.

Although he did not appear to have given the right response, he was certainly getting *confused* and *frustrated* himself. He thought hard but couldn't come up with anything else. "I don't understand, Mary, where you're going with this. I've told you what I saw, but it doesn't seem like I'm even getting warm. How am I supposed to guess what those expressions mean?"

Mary smiled and looked intently at Jerry in a way that made him feel uncomfortable. "You don't have to guess, Jerry. All you need to do is tell me what you saw; simplest thing in the world. So far, you haven't told me anything you saw. All you have done is given me a bunch of interpretations of what you think my expressions and actions meant to you. But that isn't what I asked. I asked what you *saw*." She paused for a moment and then continued, "There's a reason I have *two* colored pens in my hand."

Jerry just sat scratching his head and looking perplexed, and then suddenly it dawned on him what she was asking. "You stomped your foot," he said.

Mary wrote *stomped foot* in green.

"You snapped your fingers," he added.

Mary wrote *snapped fingers* in green.

"You looked at the floor. You shook your head. You pressed your lips together like this," he said, imitating how Mary had pursed her lips.

"Slow down!" she laughed as she wrote each of these in green. "Now you're beginning to understand, Jerry. All of the items in red are what we call interpretations," and she wrote the word *interpretation* in large letters in red. "All of the items in green are what we call observations," she said as she wrote the word *observation* in green. "An observation is defined as what each person would agree they saw, assuming they had the physical ability to see what I was doing and sufficient time to observe it. An interpretation could be anything depending on how one internalizes the information one has observed. Interpretations are influenced by many factors including one's beliefs, one's biases, emotional state, and, very important, how much time one spends observing and how intently one observes. About the closest you could come to interpreting what I was doing accurately would be to say that I was *acting* in order to prove a point, but even that would be a guess," Mary explained as she placed the two pens back on the flip chart and sat down in one of the large chairs facing Jerry.

Jerry shook his head and said, "But isn't it normal for us to interpret what we see? What is the point of observing something if we don't try to figure out what it means?"

"Absolutely," Mary replied. "The problem is that too often we are too quick to take an observation and interpret what it means. My guess is that in most cases we spend ten percent of our brain power observing and ninety percent interpreting what it means. In the example I just did, you were at one hundred percent interpretation. Until I prodded you, you didn't tell me a single thing that you saw."

"But again, isn't this natural?" Jerry asked.

"It may be considered 'natural' in the sense that is how most people function. But it leads to a lot of the wrong conclusions. If we spent ninety percent of the time observing and ten percent interpreting, we would understand the world and the people in it a lot better and learn one heck of a lot more."

"But if interpreting is so natural and so easy, how do we force ourselves to observe?" Jerry asked.

"That's exactly how we do it, Jerry. We force ourselves. The key is to turn off our internal dialogue, the *voice* in our head that tells us what everything means. This voice is the source of most of our problems. We must try our best to watch, listen, and feel without hanging on values or ratings or file what we see it in some cubbyhole that reinforces our belief. We simply observe. Naturally, at some point we will interpret what it means. But true seeing, like empathic listening, is done without interpreting, initially. The reason I am sharing this with you, Jerry, is that I suspect, and I'm interpreting now, that your judgments about your garden and those of your boss and the company you work for and maybe, as of late, your life in general are lacking in sufficient *observation*."

Jerry was taken aback by this assertion. "Well, I, uh . . ." and he thought for a few moments and said, "Maybe you're right. I'll need to think about it some more."

"All of organizational gardening is very basic, Jerry," said Mary. "And by basic, I mean it is foundational to the way we see the world, to the way we behave as individuals and then, as we behave when interacting with others. As an engineer, you know the stronger the foundation, the more stable that which is built on top will be. These foundational principles support all of the things we do: our job, our interaction with others, our personal lives, everything. And the most basic is our observation of the external world through our five senses; sight, feel, sound, taste, and smell. Let's call them 'windows' into our brains. Our conscious mind opens and closes these windows. When we were very young, up to the age of one or so, all we did was observe and act, then gradually we began to interpret what it all means. Of course, this was necessary. The ability to interpret observations of the external world in a rational way is called intelligence.

"It takes only one occurrence of placing your hand on a hot surface to know that *hot* means *hurt*. So we observe a hot surface and we interpret, 'Don't touch.' But as we grow older, we take it too far. We see someone of a particular race or gender or age, and because we have seen someone of that particular race or gender or age act a certain way before, we assume, we interpret, that all people of that age or gender will act the same. We may be right, but in so many cases we are wrong. So sharpening our skills of observation can only help us learn. It may be the single most important thing we can do to increase our capacity to learn. Observation is the source of all knowledge, and to observe without interpreting may be the highest form of intelligence."

Jerry sat in silence, slowly nodding his head. "I think I am beginning to understand what you mean, Mary. And you would think for someone with a science background, good observation would be second nature. I think I do apply it in the way I solve problems at work, but then I tend to ignore it in my relations with others and in my own behavior." Jerry sat quietly for a few more moments, pondering what Mary had said, and then asked, "So where do I go from here?"

"My interpretation of what I have observed," Mary said laughing, "is that you should go back and observe more intently what is happening in your garden and your job. What do you think?"

"I have to agree, Mary," Jerry said, shaking his head. "Any suggestions for how I can make it any easier?"

"Try to look, listen, and feel without that voice in the back of your head, that *internal dialogue,* kicking in too soon and telling you what it means. The main key to observation is turning off our internal dialogue. At the same time, look for patterns. And by patterns I mean similarities of occurrences in your garden in a physiological sense with what may be reflected in a psychological sense in your behavior with yourself and others. Make sense?"

"I think so," Jerry said, not sure whether it did or not. "Let me mull it over and give it a try. By the way, I met one of your employees last weekend, Jennifer; she seems like she is up on all of this organizational gardening stuff, too. She explained what that tomato on your shirt stands for."

"Yeah, Jennifer mentioned you had stopped by. She is a very impressive young lady. Some time ago she moved in with me and has been renting a room while she looks for a place to live."

"What a lucky girl. Well, I better be going and let you get back to potting roses. Thank you for the insights, Mary. I'll be talking to you again soon, I'm sure."

"Anytime, Jerry; it'll be my pleasure," she said as she returned to her rosebushes.

Chapter Five

Starting to See

*F*or the next two weeks Jerry tried his best to apply what Mary had shared with him about observation, both at work and at home. He stared at the plants for long periods of time but was unable to come up with anything new. He did note that several of the leaves on the tomato plants were turning yellow. He had been watering the plants frequently because he didn't want any of them to wilt like the one he forgot to water before. Thinking he wasn't watering them enough, he gave them a little more water just to be safe. What could it hurt? The soil seemed pretty wet, but it had been unusually warm lately, so maybe they needed some more. Why would the leaves turn yellow if it wasn't from a lack of water? The grass in the neighbors' lawn across the street was completely yellow, and he never saw them watering.

The application of Mary's suggestions was even more difficult at work, particularly when he was interacting with Andy Mills. Turning off that internal dialogue, as Mary called the silent voice in his head, was a challenge. Whenever he was around Mills, all he could think about was what an ass Mills was. As Mills talked to him, his internal dialogue would be focused on the rebuttal he would use if Mills would only shut up. But Andy was an artist at monopolizing the conversation and he made Jerry feel so inferior that when Mills finally stopped talking, Jerry usually didn't have the courage to tell him what he was thinking.

During one meeting with Mills he noticed that he was wearing a particularly nice tie. Mills prided himself on being a snazzy dresser, but sometimes Jerry thought that he dressed in a very tacky way. But this time Jerry liked the tie, so he told him so. The rest of the meeting Mills was unusually nice to him. Was there something he should note in this behavior? He sure wasn't going to compliment Mills on his trashy-looking clothes every time they had a meeting just so Mills would be nice to him. One thing Jerry refused to do was suck up to management.

This attempt to apply this observation stuff was starting to give Jerry a headache. It took too much concentration, and it didn't seem to be providing any insights. Two weeks after he last met with Mary, Jerry had nothing to show for his observation efforts. His garden seemed to be dying despite his attempt to show his love by religiously watering it every day. He was starting to slip back into that feeling of ineptitude he had when he first went to see Mary. It was Friday night (TGIF—so what?), but he didn't feel like going out. He watched some TV and went to bed early.

After trying to get back into a novel he had been reading on and off for over a year, Jerry fell into a deep sleep. Early in the morning, just before sunrise, he had the most unusual dream. He dreamed he was meeting with Mills on the McCabe project, but when he entered Mills' office he noticed that he was wearing some kind of "frog" costume, or maybe it was a large frog with Mills' face. Either way, the frog/Mills silently motioned for Jerry to sit down and then pulled a large hose from behind his desk and started spraying it full force into Jerry's face. Jerry tried to get up and tell him to stop but was unable to do either. The water kept coming full force until Jerry thought he was going to drown, and then he woke up!

He lay there for a few moments, unable to believe he had dreamed something so ridiculous, but the image was still vivid in his mind. He could almost feel and taste the water hitting his face. Then all of a sudden something came to him. He jumped out of bed and ran to the book on gardening Mary gave him. He quickly thumbed to the index and looked for the word *watering*. He opened to one of the pages indicated and read the following:

All plants need water, but the amount and frequency of watering varies from plant to plant. For plants like

tomatoes, good drainage is essential. The soil should be allowed to become dry between watering. This encourages the plant's root growth. Too much or too little water can kill or stunt the growth of a plant and cause the tomatoes to be mealy and to split. One rule of thumb is that if the leaves close to the plants roots are brown or yellow, the plant may be receiving too much water. If the leaves at the tips of the plants stems are yellow, it may indicate a lack of water. Particularly with tomatoes, as the plant's root system develops there is less need to water as frequently. Of course there are other reasons why a plant's leaves may turn yellow. Refer to section on plant disease and fertilizing for more information.

That's it," Jerry thought. "I've loved my plants to death! And Mills sometimes loves me to death, although I doubt he would put it in the category of 'love'. "

The sun had just come up, so Jerry quickly dressed and walked outside to take a closer look at his garden. He felt the soil and found it sopping wet. The tomato plants' leaves were a yellowish brown close to the base of the plant. All except one! Jerry hadn't noticed before, perhaps because he had not really been observing, but one of the tomato plants in the back seemed to be doing fine. Its leaves were a dark green color and it was taller and healthier looking than the others. In fact, it had several small yellow flowers, and a couple appeared to be starting to form a tomato fruit. The soil around the plant was slightly damp, but definitely not anywhere as wet as the other plants. Jerry asked himself how he could have missed this plant; obviously because it was in the back. And luckily so! Otherwise he might have overwatered and loved it to death, too.

Jerry thought back on his encounters with his boss. Was this the parallel Mary was referring to? Although one wouldn't call it love or even affection, Mills' help when Jerry didn't need it might be compared to Jerry watering his plants when they didn't need watering. The leaves turning yellow from overwatering could be similar to Jerry's feeling of dejection and frustration when Mills insisted on giving him advice when Jerry didn't need it. Jerry had the same feeling when Mills didn't help him when he did need it. Jerry felt that there was a parallel here with the plant's leaves turning yellow due to a *lack* of water and turning yellow due to over watering. It was an interesting thought and an exciting observation.

Jerry couldn't wait to tell Mary what he had discovered. But was it too soon? Last time he had jumped to the wrong conclusions. Jerry went back over his observations. No. This time he was onto something. Of course, that was why Mary asked him to go back and rethink what he was doing; he had been killing his plants. And perhaps his job, too! Wasn't it strange, though, that she hadn't just told him so? Was self-discovery a more powerful route?

The nursery opened at 7:30 on the weekends. Jerry stopped to get a Starbucks on the way and sipped it as he waited for the nursery to open. A lot of customers came in early in the morning. Perhaps not surprising. It was springtime; time to plant, time to start anew!

When the doors opened, Jerry walked in. The first employee he saw was Jennifer. She greeted him with a warm smile and said, "Well, look who's here. Hey, Jerry! You're becoming a regular around here. How ya been?"

"Not bad, Jennifer, and you?"

"Great! Can I help you with something?"

"I'm looking for Mary again. Is she here?"

"No, she won't be in until later. But if you're looking for some more plants, I can help you find them."

"No. I need to talk to her about some of that organizational gardening stuff. I have been trying to sharpen my observation skills, and I just had the most amazing discovery. Actually, it was in a dream last night. I wanted to share it with her to see if I am on the right track."

"You can come back around 10, or if you'd like, I would be happy to hear what you've experienced. I love that stuff and try really hard to remember my dreams."

Jerry wasn't sure if he wanted to share what had happened to him with Jennifer. He felt very comfortable talking to Mary about anything, but he didn't know Jennifer that well. But as he looked at her he intuitively felt that it was OK, so he related what Mary had asked him to do and the frustration he had felt trying to observe and find parallels and patterns. He described what he had done to his plants, and as he did, Jennifer smiled in a way that was not mocking; it was but more like she understood. He described his dream, and Jennifer laughed as he related the encounter with Mills.

"So you see I had no clue until I had this dream. Then all of a sudden it was clear. Mary talked about creating an environment that allows plants to grow and the importance of observation, but I was going on preconceived ideas of when help is needed, even though I had experienced the exact opposite at work!"

"Your insight is correct," Jennifer said, slowly nodding her head. "The interesting part is that it came to you in a dream rather than when you were awake. I've never had that happen to me. All of my 'aha's' happened when I was awake. It is unusual for these insights to be revealed in a dream. It's an excellent example of how when we plant seeds in our subconscious, they may sprout at the most unusual times."

"Plant seeds in our subconscious? What do you mean?" Jerry asked.

"When we have been thinking about something a lot, take for example the solution to a crossword puzzle hint, and we leave it alone for awhile, at some point the answer may jump into our conscious mind. Planting seeds in our subconscious is one of the most important parts of self-cultivation, perhaps the most important part."

"Self-cultivation," Jerry repeated, looking confused.

"It's an organizational gardening term for self-improvement," Jennifer responded. "Normally, after planting these seeds, as you did in your quest for parallels between observations of your garden and your work, a period of rest is needed; much like when we exercise heavily, we need to take some time off before stressing those muscles again. During this period our subconscious may be working on the solution even though our conscious mind is unaware. It's almost like our conscious mind needs to rest, or maybe our subconscious does. Our conscious mind is always feeding ideas to our subconscious, but our subconscious doesn't care; it acts on whatever it gets, junk or jewels or maybe something neutral like the solution to a crossword puzzle. The magic happens when we feed our subconscious jewels, positive pictures of who we want to be or what we want to accomplish."

"Interesting," Jerry said. "I'm sure I've had this happen to me before, but didn't really think about it. There's one thing that I'm confused about, though. I now see the parallel between the plants and my interactions at work, but I don't know what to do about it. Well, I do know what to do about my garden; I'm going to cut back on the watering. Hopefully those poor plants will recover. I don't feel I have the same control over the situation at work, however. If my boss wants to tell me what to do when I already know, or if he chooses to ignore me when I need help, that's his prerogative. Am I not at his mercy?"

"Yes, if you want to plant those seeds, you certainly may." Jennifer responded, shaking her head. "But I would put it in the category of 'junk'. You need to cultivate some jewels instead."

Looking offended, Jerry asked "What do you mean?"

"Let's use the example of your garden, OK? Let's pretend that those tomato plants are *thinking tomatoes."* as she grasped the tomato patch on her shirt between her thumb and her forefinger. "That is, let's assume they have a brain and are able to get up and walk or even talk. How do you think they might have reacted when you tried to drown them?"

"Why, they would tell me to stop, and if I didn't stop they would get up and plant themselves somewhere else, or maybe they would grab the hose and take it away from me," he said, laughing at what he thought was a ridiculous comparison. "But all that hypothetical stuff is fine; however, last time I checked, tomatoes can neither think nor move on their own."

"But you can, can't you, Jerry?"

Jerry was silent for a few moments as the significance of what Jennifer asked him sunk in. Then he said, "Yeah, you're right. I can. Only it's not so simple. Mills is my boss. He may be a total ass, but he's my boss. Lately, people have been laid off right and left, and I don't want to be the next one. The phrase around work is 'Don't make waves.'"

"Do you believe that your company would be better off if your boss left you alone when you knew what to do, but helped you when you didn't?"

"Absolutely," Jerry responded.

"If it were your company, that is, if you owned the company, wouldn't you want this?"

"Absolutely!" he responded again.

"Wouldn't you want all employees in your company to communicate with their bosses and tell them when they are being over- or under-watered, to, as you say, make waves, or would you prefer they act like brainless tomatoes?"

"I would want them to speak up if they were being treated improperly, of course."

"Are you saying, then, that you're not the type of person you would want working in the company if you owned it?"

"No, that's not what I'm saying." Jerry stammered. Jennifer seemed to have a way of seeing through him. He was silent a few moments, and then he hung his head and said, "Yeah, I guess that is what I'm saying. I'm not sure how to approach Mills, though. In the past when I've tried to argue with him, it only got worse."

Just as Jennifer was getting ready to reply, she looked over Jerry's shoulder and saw Mary walking over to where they were standing.

"What are you two up to?" Mary asked, greeting them with a big smile.

"Hello, Mary," they said in unison.

Jennifer added, "Jerry has had some significant insights, and he was sharing them with me."

"I'd love to hear about them," Mary said.

Jennifer looked at her watch and said, "Oh, I was supposed to meet with John fifteen minutes ago. I'd better run. I'm sure Mary would like to hear what you've discovered, Jerry, if she has time."

"For sure," Mary said.

"I'll see you later, Jerry," as she took off across the nursery.

Chapter Six

The "Want to," the "How to," and the Birds and the Bees

W hat a clever young lady," Jerry volunteered as they watched Jennifer disappear behind several large potted trees.

"Yes, she certainly is," Mary said. "But tell me, what has been happening with you?"

Jerry related the problems with his plants, the dream about his boss, and what he had discovered. He described what Jennifer discussed with him about self-cultivation and planting seeds in the subconscious.

"When you walked up, we were talking about the parallel between a thinking tomato and how people should act in an organization. I think Jennifer thinks I'm a dumb tomato," Jerry said, looking at the ground.

"How so?" Mary asked.

Jerry told her about his frustration with Andy, who treated him so inconsistently, sometimes helping him when he needed no help and ignoring him completely when he needed it.

"I understand why I need to act differently, but I don't know what to do," Jerry moaned.

"I suggest we look at another foundational concept, something you probably know intuitively but may not be aware of its importance. Like observation, it is something that is critically important, but also something we tend to forget."

"And what's that?" Jerry asked.

"To learn something, we have two basic needs; first, we need to be motivated to act. We call this the *want to*. And second, we need to gradually get to know how to do whatever it is we are trying to learn. We call this the *how to*. Since we start out knowing nothing about a particular task or endeavor, normally all we have is the motivation, the 'want to'. In some cases we have neither, particularly when we are given something to do that we've made up our minds we don't want to do, say some dirty, undesirable, or unpopular task. Assuming we have the motivation, our first need is to learn how to do whatever it is we are trying to learn. Sometimes this comes easily, but in many cases, particularly with something that is difficult to learn, it doesn't. In this case we may lose our motivation. This can happen for a lot of reasons, perhaps because we start making mistakes or we fail completely, or someone criticizes us, or whatever. Our wonderful brain takes over, and instead of being excited about it, we become discouraged and disillusioned. We get down on ourselves, which makes learning even more difficult. At this stage, many times we check out, we give up, we quit, telling ourselves sometimes that it's the rational way out. Other times we may get further down on ourselves because we did quit."

"Obviously we are able to learn a lot of difficult tasks," Jerry said. "How do we get through it?"

"First, we have to dispel the feeling of being discouraged. Replace it with a feeling of 'I can,' a feeling of self-confidence; rekindle the excitement and motivation we had initially. There are many ways to do this; talking to someone about it is one of the best ways. Our burdens are never as great when we share them with someone else, particularly when that someone is able to empathize with us, sort of like, I trust, what we are doing now and what you were doing talking with Jennifer. But there are countless other ways—books, encounter groups, self-help classes, and so on. Ultimately though, we must find this support within ourselves. That comes with practice and an increasingly positive image of who we want to be in every situation in which we are trying to learn or change. After we rekindle the motivation, we need to find the best process for getting the 'how to'. Here again, there are a multitude of sources. It could be our boss, or a peer, or a subject-matter expert, a mentor, a class, a book, or, often, it's just experimenting on our own. If a person is a self-leader, a self-starter, a thinking tomato, he will fulfill these needs in the sense of finding a way on his own."

"I think I'm starting to see what you mean, Mary. So, if Mills isn't helping me when I need it, I need to either somehow get him to assist me or find some other source of help, whether it's getting motivated or learning how to get whatever I need."

"Exactly, Jerry."

"But how about the situation I'm in on this one project at work where Mills insists on giving me advice when I don't need it?"

"What would a thinking tomato do?" Mary asked.

"Probably explain that his help isn't needed."

"Well, you have your answer."

"Look, Mary. I have a hard time being around Mills. He's such a dope. I've tried talking to him and it never works. He just cuts me off and never listens. And I'm not about to suck up to him. One thing I'm not is a hypocrite."

"Jerry, I'm not suggesting you suck up to anyone. Your boss is like most people on this earth; he has both good points and bad points, just like you and I. If you focus on the bad, you will never get anywhere. Have you ever wondered why plants have flowers?" she asked, picking up a small lavender plant sitting next to her.

"To attract bees, of course, in order to pollinate the flower and produce seeds," Jerry responded, wondering where Mary was going with this. "I know about the birds and the bees, but so what?"

"Do you believe the flower is being hypocritical, seducing poor bees with sweet aromas and pretty colors?"

"No, eh . . . I . . . eh . . ." he stammered.

"You see, Jerry, the flower and the bee have a symbiotic relationship, a win/win relationship. The bee gets the nectar, the flower gets pollinated. Both win. Each helps the other. But if the bee killed the flower, or if the flower killed the bee, eventually both would cease to exist. Why is this different from your relationship with your boss? A positive relationship and mutual benefit increases the probability that both of you will continue to be productive at work. Win/win relationships require mutual benefit; both of you can take the first steps to make this happen, but, it appears the ball is in your court."

"So you think I need to be more 'flower-like' when I deal with Mills?" Jerry asked.

"Yes, I definitely do. There are two parts to the flower/bee relationship. First, there must be an attraction; something must cause the bee to want to go to the flower. The flower does this with color and aroma. The beauty of the flower serves no function to the bee, I suspect, other than attraction. Bees don't pick flowers and take them back to the hive to admire. Second, there must be something for the bee once it chooses a particular flower. Of course this is the nectar. You may have at one time or another been wearing a very colorful shirt and had a bee fly up to you, but it realized that there was no nectar, so it flew away. The same attraction and value must exist in our relationship with others. You first need to create a positive atmosphere between you and the other person. You can't do this by seeing that person as an ass, or an idiot, or a dope. He will sense it in your body language. You have to look for his positive qualities, which you will find most people have, if you observe. After you establish the rapport, you need to be brave enough to say what you think, focusing whenever possible on observables rather than interpretations. My guess is that if your boss was psychic, that is, he really knew what you thought of him, he would treat you a lot differently. But since mind reading may not be his forte, it's as much up to you to give him feedback as it is for the thinking tomato to yell 'Stop!' when someone tries to unknowingly drown it. Metaphorically, it's the same."

Jerry watched a bee fly to a lavender plant. It paused on a flower for only a few seconds, doing whatever bees do, before flying off to either another flower or to its hive. Jerry nodded slowly and said, "I see what you mean, Mary. It makes so much sense when you put it that way. Mills hasn't been trying to 'drown' me. I've been doing it to myself."

"Think about it, Jerry, and then try to put it into practice. Observe his good points and focus on your mutual benefits. You may not get it exactly right the first time, but if you keep trying, you will. The initial step of the journey is the most important."

Jerry looked at his watch and said, "Thanks, Mary. This has been very helpful. Thanks for being so patient with me. I'm sorry I've been such a bonehead. And tell Jennifer I appreciate her help, also. I'll get out of your hair now and let you go to work. Thanks again."

"You're welcome. But there's no need to apologize, for what, learning? If you would like to continue learning about organizational gardening, why not come over for dinner next weekend on Saturday? I'll invite a couple other people from the nursery, including Jennifer. By talking with them you'll get several other perspectives. And I would love for you to meet them."

"Sounds great, Mary."

"Say about 7:00 or so?"

"I'm looking forward to it already. I haven't been to your place in a while, and I'm very interested in exploring what you've been saying more. Take care, Mary," he said as he walked off to his car.

Chapter Seven

Dinner at Mary's

*M*ary lived on three acres of land on the outskirts of the city. A long drive wound up to her house, a contemporary structure that looked like something out of *Home Décor* magazine. Large majestic oaks along each side of the drive formed a canopy of green. The grounds were immaculate with flowers blooming everywhere. At the same time, there was a wild, random, natural feel to the landscaping that gave it the appearance of not having been touched by humans.

Jerry parked in front beside several other vehicles he did not recognize. He assumed the other associates from the nursery had already arrived. He rang the doorbell and Jennifer answered. "Hello, Jennifer," Jerry said.

"Hey, Jerry! Come in. Mary is busy cooking, so she asked me to get the door. Not a bad place, huh? She may have mentioned that I've been renting a room from her until I find another place. I say 'renting,' but she's charging me just a pittance, I don't have a lot of desire to move. To be honest, I haven't been looking too hard." She laughed. "Come on back. Mary invited a couple of other people from the nursery to join us. They're all outside on the patio."

Jerry followed Jennifer through the house. He couldn't help notice how the house was decorated with antiques, modern furniture and a variety of colorful, interesting objects. From every angle he was assaulted with such a pleasing array of items that wherever he looked there was an appealing scene. What he remembered most was that from the moment he entered, a satisfying calmness came over him as he walked through the house. His senses were bombarded with a multitude of form and color that were very pleasing. The tiled floors gave the rooms a rustic feeling. Colorful Kilim rugs were scattered throughout the house adding an Eastern flavor. The walls were covered with a mix of modern and old paintings. A multitude of indoor green plants of all types added to the cozy feel of the space. The house was decorated in such a way that it seem to specialize in the décor of the southern areas of many lands, with a subtle leaning toward the Indian culture of the American southwest, but there were also a lot of French antiques and flavors of the Middle East, Africa, India, the Orient, and South America. He felt he could spend all day or even a week in one room and still be surprised by what he saw. As Jerry looked around he realized that Jennifer had walked to the back of the house so he followed her into a large kitchen where he found Mary, adorned in a white apron, bent over and looking intently into the oven.

"Greetings Mary," Jerry said. "I'd forgotten how beautiful your house is. Something smells fantastic!"

"Jerry!' she said looking up from the oven. " I'm so pleased you could come! Thanks. The place is starting to take on the feel of the weekend flea market in Oakland" she joked. "I need to cut back my obsession with collecting stuff. We'll see how this meal turns out" she said, closing the oven door. "I shouldn't experiment with a new recipe, but I know Jennifer and the rest will eat about anything. Jennifer, take Jerry out and introduce him to Tom and Natalie."

Jennifer led Jerry out the door of the kitchen to a large brick patio. Overhead, wooden slats covered most of the area, forming an arbor. The slats were entwined with wisteria in full bloom. The sweet smell of the wisteria mingled with that of Star jasmine growing along the edge of the patio. Large clay ceramic planters, from which a variety of plants grew, were spread throughout the patio. Numerous lit candles added to the ambiance. Jennifer walked over to several rattan sofas with large white pillows; on one of them a man and a woman sat, talking.

"Jerry, I'd like you to meet Tom and Natalie," said Jennifer.

"Hello, Natalie. Hello, Tom," said Jerry. "I recognize both of you from the nursery."

"Pleased to meet you, Jerry," said Tom. "Yes, we work there. And Natalie also lives here with Mary and Jennifer."

Jerry shook hands then sat down and commented "So both of you are living here. Mary must be running a hotel. How do you like it here?"

Natalie replied "We both love this place. I've been here about four months and Jennifer about three. The house and the grounds are so spectacular and Mary is so wonderful that it will be difficult to leave. And I think Mary likes having someone around. The house is so big that she must get lonely here by herself."

The four discussed Mary, the house, and the nursery for awhile, then Natalie turned to Jerry and said "We hear you are interested in organizational gardening"

"Yes. Both Mary and Jennifer have been telling me about it. It all sounds very interesting, but I still have a *lot* of questions. Hopefully I'll learn more about it this evening" said Jerry.

"Well, that's why were here tonight." laughed Natalie.

Mary walked up about that time and placed a plate of hors d'oeuvres on the table. "How about something to drink. Dinner will be ready soon," she said, heading back to the kitchen.

Drinks arrived, and the conversation turned to sports and politics. Jerry took an immediate liking to Tom and Natalie. Like Mary and Jennifer, both seemed unpretentious and natural. Jerry felt relaxed with these people. As Jennifer and Tom discussed about who would win the playoffs, Mary shouted that dinner was served. They would be eating outside at a table set at the opposite end of the patio. White linen, white China settings, silver, a chilled Meursault, flowers, and candles adorned the table. The company, the setting, and the pleasing aroma of food gave promise of the meal to come.

The first course was a cold soup. Tom made a toast to successful organizational gardening. The Meursault was excellent with the soup. Mary told Tom that the reason she had asked him and the others to dinner was so they could answer any questions Jerry might have about organizational gardening. She said that everyone who worked at the nursery was knowledgeable on the subject, but Jennifer, Tom, and Natalie were the experts. In fact, Natalie was the one who had originally brought the concept to her. At one time Natalie had worked for a large bioscience corporation. She had learned a lot of the ideas there but had become very frustrated with the slow pace of change. The company didn't seem to practice what it preached. Besides, she didn't really like the work she was doing, so she quit and looked for other employment. Eventually she had taken a job at the nursery and had become part of the group that researches new and different plants that might do well in the area.

Jerry was listening intently and was a little surprised by what he heard. Looking at Mary, he said, "I was under the impression that you started this and that it's unique to your company. You mean organizational gardening hasn't always been the policy at The Green Patch?"

Shaking her head, Mary responded, "No it hasn't. It used to be a lot more command and control and, how should I say, more disorganized. Often, people weren't sure what to without checking with me or one of the supervisors. I must admit that the idea didn't come to me naturally. Natalie brought it with her. Tom and Jennifer know the current culture hasn't really been in place that long."

Tom said, "Mary's right. It has always been a fun place to work, but it didn't become a great place to work until Natalie started working at the nursery and introduced the ideas to Mary. But Mary caught on immediately; she absorbed them like a sponge."

Mary interjected, "Tom's right. I became fascinated with the whole concept! The name 'organizational gardening' is something we coined. The concept that Natalie taught us was that people development is a natural process like many other natural processes, like growing plants, for instance. Unfortunately, many organizations treat people more like machines than plants. Although machines can be managed, machine management doesn't work very well on people. Our objective, and part of the ideas Natalie brought, has been to turn the traditional organizational, command-and-control pyramid upside-down. You are probably familiar with the pyramid; management or leadership is at the top, while the people who do the work that most impacts the end product or service and the customer are at the bottom or base. Traditionally, management is supposed to be 'responsible' and the workers 'responsive,' that is, the workers are suppose to check in with management and/or follow some rule book as they do their jobs. But invariably the rule book doesn't cover every circumstance, and at times it can be out of date or wrong. Nor is it either practical or effective to check with your boss about customer needs or problems very often. Frequently management is so out of the loop they don't appreciate the situation because they are not living it each day, thus they may give bad advice.

"The inverted pyramid has the workers at the top where they have the responsibility to interact favorably with the customer. By *responsibility* I mean they have the knowledge, desire, and authority to act. This is because the most important interface between a company and the customer, the one that matters, is the interface between the ordinary worker and the customer, not between upper management and the customer. When was the last time you walked into a store and were greeted by the company CEO? Never, right? You normally interact with ordinary workers, and the way they treat you determines whether you come back again. The only time we interact with management is when there is a problem. And the problem is usually a result of the workers not having the knowledge, desire, or authority to do their jobs, and then it's too late.

"The pyramid is not only turned upside-down, but it is also flattened. If the workers have the wherewithal to act, all the extra levels of management are not needed. Removing these layers improves communication up and down, not to mention the direct cost savings achieved by eliminating the levels. A critical part of management's job is to create the environment that allows workers to excel. Of course, many of the traditional management responsibilities remain, like setting the long-term vision and direction of the company, acquisition of resources, and so on, but a critical part is the organizational-gardening responsibility.

"In the inverted pyramid, management must be willing to share, sometimes give up some responsibility and power, but the workers must actively want to take on responsibility and power. They must want to fulfill their own needs rather than depend on management to do it for them, otherwise it won't work. This is where the thinking tomato comes in. A thinking tomato, by definition, is one that will fulfill its own needs: no water, go get water; customer problem, figure it out given the situation. So management, with their new organizational gardening skills in the flattened, upside-down, empowered organization is facilitating making this happen; they are the quintessential *people* gardeners, and the good ones raise prize tomatoes."

There was a period of silence as Mary and Jennifer picked up the soup bowls and carried them to the kitchen. Jerry seemed to be deep in thought as he listened to the sounds of the crickets and classical music coming from speakers somewhere on the patio. Mary and Jennifer returned with the second course, salmon filets cooked in a honey sauce with French green beans and new potatoes. Fresh glasses were filled with a fine Pinot Noir.

After everyone began eating, Mary said, "There's another reason we asked you here tonight, Jerry. I hope you don't mind, but Jennifer and I have been comparing notes. We've been looking for another apprentice to learn and practice the concepts of organizational gardening. We decided some time ago to impart this knowledge to others who might take it and, first, practice it but at some point, if it is fitting, share it with others. We have had three other 'students,' but each is on his or her own now, so we're looking for another candidate. You fit the bill perfectly. I can't explain how it happens, but we have never had to look for someone; in every case so far, they found us, just like the way you showed up at the nursery a few weeks ago. As Jennifer and I talked and discussed our interactions with you and then talked it over with Tom and Natalie, it became obvious that you are a prime candidate. You fit the criteria perfectly: you desperately need the coaching, you have proven that you catch on to the foundational concepts quickly, and you are in a position to impact others. Of course, you don't have to agree. And the only obligation is that you practice what you learn."

Jerry was very taken aback by what Mary had shared. "I feel much honored. I didn't realize all of this was going on behind the scenes." He was silent for several moments and then said, "Of course I agree to accept, but why are you doing this?"

"We've seen it work at my, excuse me, *our* nursery. We believe in it. We also believe that if we plant these seeds on a small scale, they may eventually take root, propagate, and make a positive impact on the world."

"Well, the little I have heard of what you are practicing, the world certainly needs it. I can't believe this is happening! What is the next step?" Jerry asked.

"Let me summarize where I think you are, Jerry," Natalie said. "Neither Tom nor I have been involved so far. But we've listened to Jennifer and Mary. Let me see if I understand." Natalie continued, "You've been told that you have choices and that the only right choices are to change the situation or change the way you see it. The third choice, being victimized by the situation, is a waste of time and will take you in the opposite direction of where you need to go. Once you realize you have choices, you need to understand the most foundational concept of organizational learning: the difference between observation and interpretation and the need to *choose* to spend considerably more time observing before you interpret. As you learn to give the proper credit to your five senses, it is necessary to see how you learn. This is where the 'want to' and 'how to' come into play. As you discovered trying to grow your vegetable garden, you need not only understand your needs, but you must also meet those needs yourself when they are not supplied by others. Throughout, you learn the fastest when you *see* yourself the way you would like to be; you appreciate the power of your subconscious and the job your conscious mind has in keeping it on a positive track. In your interaction with others you learn to emulate the flower, to draw the bee to you rather than chase it away. Does that pretty well sum it up, Jerry?"

"I believe so. Except I don't feel I have really learned these concepts. I need more time to put them in practice," Jerry said.

"You have all the time you need, Jerry," said Mary. "And you will certainly have a lot of opportunities. But you have an important part already; you have the *awareness,* and the first step in change is always awareness. Every day you have the chance to practice everything that Natalie covered just now, and it is through practice that you will become adept."

"All of this makes sense," said Jerry. "But the part I still don't understand is what I am supposed to do! If I can borrow your analogy, it's like a thinking tomato knowing it needs water but doesn't know where to get the water or how to hold a watering can. What exactly is self-cultivation?"

"A great question, Jerry," said Mary. "There are actually two major needs the thinking tomato has. The first is the mind-set, the belief, the desire, the commitment, the 'wanting to' that we talked about before. Without this, no matter how much of the second need one has, nothing much will happen. The second need includes the tools, the procedures, the directions, the process, the 'how to'. If the second need is not eventually filled, no matter how much one wants to, it will eventually start to fade. But when the belief and the 'want to' find the 'how to,' marvelous things begin to happen. But with that in mind, I need to clear some of these dishes off the table. I made a special chocolate mousse. Let's talk about the 'how to' over coffee and dessert."

"I can't wait!" said Jerry, looking forward to the chocolate mousse and, just maybe, further answers to his quandaries.

Chapter Eight

Personal Power—The Choice Is Yours

Jerry sat deep in thought, sipping his wine while Tom, Jennifer, and Natalie helped Mary clear the table for coffee and dessert. The analogy of the thinking tomato made a lot of sense. We human beings have a large brain, great manual dexterity, and the ability to act. Why, then, do we spend so much time whining and complaining? Mary had hit a nerve when she talked about the number of people who do nothing but complain about their situations. He knew a lot of people like that. In fact, most of his friends and his work associates fit that mold. They always had a lot of excuses why they hadn't achieved this or that or didn't have this or that. Jerry hated to listen to them whine. But wasn't that exactly what he had been doing? He had been acting like the victim, blaming his situation on his boss or the plant manager. What was it that Mary had said? *Most if not all organizations neglect the needs of some or all of their employees, most of it unintentionally.* That certainly puts a different twist on the situation. Well, as he thought about it, maybe he did have a lot of the desire, commitment, and the "want to." He could just imagine what a great place work would be if he could somehow fulfill his own needs. Now he needed to find out more about the "how to."

"A penny for your thoughts," Jennifer said, setting down a large silver pot.

The aroma of freshly brewed coffee filled the air. Tom arrived with a tray of porcelain demitasse cups and saucers. Natalie carried a tray with five *pots de crème*, small cups with lids, most probably containing the chocolate mousse. After everyone was seated, Mary commented that the quantity of mousse was small but very potent. She indicated there was more if anyone wanted some. Jerry took a small spoonful. *Heavenly,* he thought.

Realizing Jennifer had asked him what he had been thinking, Jerry said, "I have to confess that when it comes to victims, I'm one of the worst. All I've been thinking about is how unfortunate I am. I've blamed everyone but myself for my situation at work. I'm like a tomato that can think but has decided to do nothing but die. What you have taught me so far has been very helpful."

"You're not alone, Jerry," said Mary. "All of us fall into the victim mentality some time or other. Life can be very challenging. Often we feel at the mercy of the world. And sometimes it feels like everyone is dumping on us. However, in just about every case, we can do something about it. We have a great gift, the gift of choice. And as we said before, only two good choices exist: changing the way we look at a situation or changing the situation itself. No other correct alternatives exist. Unfortunately, too many people do neither. They just sit around complaining and feeling sorry for themselves."

"Yeah," Jerry said. "Like when I get stuck in heavy traffic. I tend to get in a bad mood and start cursing at the other drivers. My only real choice is to choose not to worry about it. I mean, what other choice do I have? Walking away from the car? Abandoning it on the freeway? It's not that easy to do, though. I mean not being a victim, not leaving my car on the freeway," he said, laughing. "I hope I can change my behavior in situations at work and elsewhere. I'm anxious to try."

"And we're anxious to help you, Jerry," said Jennifer. "We'll pass on the same knowledge each of us received working at The Green Patch. We're fortunate to work for a company that believes the greatest gift an employee can receive is the gift of learning to take responsibility and see life as a place of possibilities and opportunities rather than a prison of limitations. Natalie was the transition figure for us. But someone taught her. Not figuring it out on your own is understandable, but to *not* pursue a life of responsibility after being exposed to it is unforgivable. The choice, however, is yours."

"I'm all ears," said Jerry, leaning forward.

"First of all, self-cultivation is one hundred percent about you," said Natalie, setting down her empty mousse cup. "And it starts by *you* realizing what you have going for yourself. Since the main stuff that keeps us motivated, the stuff that fuels our actions, is the 'want to,' you must try to saturate yourself with an unwavering belief in yourself. You can do this by focusing on your personal power. Later, we will share with you the Seven P's and how they impact you."

"My 'personal power'," Jerry said, laughing. "The seven peas. First tomatoes, then peas. Are they *petit pois* peas? What's next, corn?"

"Very funny, Jerry," said Natalie. "I'm talking about the letter P, not the vegetable. You'll find out about these concepts later. Seriously, personal power is about how we can use our talents to influence others to help us fulfill our needs. It's about using that influence to not only obtain our needs but to make the world a better place. It's very foundational. Using the analogy of growing plants, our personal power is like the nutrients that are already in the soil. They are there for the plant to utilize if it develops the right root system. Personal power is there to be tapped at any time once we have the awareness to recognize it, develop it, and access it."

"Can you give me an example of 'personal power'?" Jerry asked.

"Well, rather than me giving you examples, why don't you come up with some yourself? Make a list of ways you are able to influence other people. Here's a sheet of paper and a pencil. Why don't the rest of you do the same?" Natalie asked as she reached into a bag and passed paper and pencils around.

"I'm still confused," Jerry said. "Can you give me a hint?"

"It could be anything associated with you: your knowledge and skills, your personal characteristics, or how you interact with other people—anything you have going for yourself," Natalie responded.

What do I have going for myself? Jerry asked himself. *Well, at work I manage several projects*, so he wrote down *project manager*. He thought some more. *I have a degree in electrical engineering, and I use what I learned in school at work all of the time*, so he wrote *electrical engineer*. He thought and thought but couldn't come up with any other ways he could influence others. He looked around at Jennifer, Tom, and Natalie and noticed that each had ten items. He felt embarrassed and a little stupid with only two.

Natalie asked, "How are you doing, Jerry?"

"Not very well," Jerry responded. "My list is pretty short. I guess I don't have much ability to influence others. Maybe that's why work has been going the way it has."

Natalie said, "You're probably being too hard on yourself, Jerry. I know you have a lot more than ten ways you can influence others. Personal power encompasses many aspects of each person. Unfortunately, people too often think only of position power, which is our ability to influence others because of name, title, or place in the hierarchy of the organization. I see you wrote *project manager* on your list. If you didn't have that title, would you still have the same influence?"

"Probably not," Jerry said. "It seems like most of the power *is* position power. If you are not one of the bosses, you don't have much influence."

"It may seem like that," said Mary, "but there are too many examples of people who had no position power influencing large numbers of people, even nations. Think about Gandhi or Martin Luther King and what they were able to accomplish with no position power. The problem is that most people don't realize how much power they actually have, so they don't try to use it. They envision themselves being powerless; they plant that seed in their subconscious, and that is what they become. As Natalie describes some of the other sources of personal power, you will begin to see how much influence you have."

"Right," said Natalie. "Another source of power is knowledge, the ability to influence others based on what you know. Examples include having a degree or certificate, being a subject-matter expert, or being exceptionally knowledgeable in any particular subject. I see you wrote *electrical engineer* on your list. This would certainly apply. Do you have any other special knowledge?"

"Actually, now that I think about it, I do." said Jerry. "I know a lot about computer hardware and I consider myself a sort of computer wiz. I built my home computer from scratch, and it works better than the one I have at work. Frequently when people at work are having problems with their computers, they come to me. And I have written some special programs to make some of the project work easier to track."

Natalie said, "Sounds like you have two items to add to your list: computer hardware knowledge and programming. Items like programming more appropriately come under skills. But there tends to be a lot of overlap in the power of our knowledge and skills. It matters less what you call it than the realization that you have it. It's about having a skill, that is, being able to apply the knowledge and use that ability to influence others. Your examples are good. Other examples would include being a good coach, facilitator, or mechanic."

"1 had never thought of these skills as enhancing our personal power," said Jerry. "It's just something I know how to do. How can it be used to influence others?"

Jennifer, who had been sitting quietly, interjected, "Most people don't see it as power. But think about a time when someone knew something that you didn't, and you needed the information or skill. How did you treat them?"

"I see," said Jerry. "I would probably treat them really well, and I might do a special favor for them or give them something or even pay them. At least I would think I owed them one, and whenever they were in need, I'd be ready and willing to help them."

"Exactly," said Jennifer. "You probably wouldn't share your knowledge with someone for the specific purpose of having someone owe you one; nevertheless that payback would exist, and that adds to your personal power through a form of mutual obligation, like the symbiotic flower-and-bee relationship. You help me and I'll help you."

"I'm beginning to understand this power thing," Jerry said thoughtfully. "What's another example?"

"There are a lot of examples," Natalie said. "Take for example attributes such as good people skills, strength of character, shedding self-importance, being disciplined, inspirational, persistent, passionate, a visionary, charismatic, a good listener, or having a good sense of humor or being attractive."

Jerry was adding to his list while Natalie talked. "OK, I think I've ten now. I've added persistence, good interpersonal skills, being well organized, disciplined, a good sense of humor, and I feel that I'm a good listener."

"I think we all agree that you are not only a good listener but an excellent listener. Don't be embarrassed, but when we were in the kitchen, we were discussing how attentive you are. Being a good listener is one of the most valuable personal characteristics we can have, because it influences our ability to learn, and one of the most powerful ways to learn is by listening intently and with an open mind, particularly when we focus on the observables."

"Thank you very much," Jerry said modestly. "You have any more examples of personal power?"

Natalie said, "Yes, and it is perhaps the most important one. It's about the relationships we develop with others. Very often it is thought of as knowing someone who is influential or having a close relationship with someone related to someone influential, like being married to the boss's daughter. To many of us, this shortcut is offensive. The most important source of personal power is the way we interact with other people, like keeping promises, admitting errors, listening empathetically, always having win/win agreements, being helpful to others, and doing things for others. Sooner or later, all power comes down to the interaction of people through relationships. It doesn't matter how much we know or what great skills we have, if we don't know how to interact with others in a positive way, eventually this power will be of no use. Notice the similarity with the bee/flower relationship. Positive, ongoing, mutually beneficial relationships are like the nectar for the bee's honey and pollination for the plant."

Mary said, "Thanks very much for the review, Natalie. We should continuously build our personal power, Jerry. The more power we have, the better we feel about ourselves. We become more confident as we are able to use our power to influence others to get what we need. Our confidence in ourselves spirals in a positive direction. And you will see how important it is when you are exposed to the Seven P's."

"How do we build our personal power?" Jerry asked.

"There are several ways," said Tom. "Let's take knowledge, for instance. We increase our knowledge by reading books, magazines, newspapers, and journals, taking classes, going back to school, by listening openly to different points of view or by getting out of our comfort zone and trying something new, in short, by making continuous learning an integral part of our lives. And the more we focus on increasing our skills of observation, the more we learn."

"Hmmm," said Jerry, slowly nodding with understanding.

"And," said Jennifer, "we can improve our relationships every time we interact with anyone. That opportunity presents itself many times a day. Simply by keeping promises, admitting errors, listening empathetically, and doing things for others, we are seen as honest, caring, and helpful. When we are in need, there is a greater probability someone will be there to help us out. Oh, and one more very important item: never speak ill of anyone, particularly when that person is not present. Petty gossip about people generally erodes power and can not only destroy a relationship with the person we are talking about but also those we are sharing it with. They are likely to think we gossip and talk about them the same way when they're not around."

"Those are very good points, Jennifer," said Jerry. "Thanks a lot."

"And remember this," said Natalie. "When we are increasing our skills or learning something new, the mind doesn't know the difference between reality and imagination."

Jerry, puzzled, asked, "Imagination? Reality? What are you talking about now?"

Jennifer said, "It's about planting those seeds of our success in our subconscious. Let's say you have a big presentation to make to your boss and other executives at your company."

"Actually, I have," interrupted Jerry.

"And," continued Jennifer, "you've been dreading this presentation for some time."

"Bingo again."

"Even though you know the material cold, you visualize yourself being put on the spot and not having the answer, or stuttering, or making a fool of yourself or whatever. When you imagine yourself screwing up, you are programming your subconscious, that is, planting seeds that will grow into weeds. The subconscious doesn't care what information your conscious mind inputs; it will be influenced by whatever it is directed to believe. So when the big presentation comes around, you have already convinced yourself that you will fail, and the likelihood is that that is exactly what will happen. On the other hand, if you visualize yourself succeeding, feeling confident, answering the questions superbly, speaking coherently, and so on, you are much more likely to behave that way. When we combine practice and pre-work, that is, thorough preparation, with a vision of ourselves succeeding, we greatly increase the probability we will."

Tom interjected, "This applies to any task, and it isn't just speculation. There have been numerous studies that show how powerful positive visualization of yourself, through imagination, can impact your actual performance. Consider the Olympics. Every one of those superb athletes sees himself or herself crossing the finish line first, jumping the farthest, lifting the most weight, or being first in winning the gold. Otherwise they wouldn't have made it that far. Of course they still have to train and practice a lot. Positive images alone will not fill the bill, but the very act of positive focus somehow creates opportunities that we weren't even aware of."

"What we're really talking about here is the most important relationship we have," said Mary.

"You mean our relationship with ourselves?" Jerry almost shouted. "That's it, isn't it?"

"Absolutely, Jerry," said Mary. "Until we have the power to influence our own behavior, it is difficult to influence the behavior of others. Just like we can't effectively lead others until we learn how to lead ourselves. There are many ways we can influence our own behavior, such as by using our imagination to visualize ourselves succeeding, being honest with ourselves, and giving ourselves positive feedback."

"Giving ourselves positive feedback? What do you mean?" asked Jerry.

Mary responded, "Eighty percent of the time the average person is giving himself or herself negative feedback, mentally saying things like 'I can't,' 'I'm powerless,' 'I'm not deserving,' 'I'm not smart enough,' 'I don't have the strength, the endurance, the will,' and so on. After a while, the person starts believing it, and it becomes a self-fulfilling prophecy. It's one of the major forces that erode our power. And we do it to ourselves!"

"How do we stop doing it?" asked Jerry.

"We simply stop doing it," said Mary. "Whenever we catch ourselves being negative, telling ourselves things like 'I can't' or 'I won't be able to' or 'I'm probably going to look stupid or screw up' or 'I'm not worthy,' we tell ourselves the opposite: 'I can' or 'I'm going to look great' or 'I'm really looking forward to giving the presentation' or 'I am deserving.' I say 'we simply stop,' but initially it may not be so easy. We're so habituated to being negative that it takes significant effort to catch ourselves and start reprogramming our internal dialogue and our subconscious with positive beliefs. But the effort is well worth it. Possibly, in addition to spending more time observing, it is the most worthwhile effort we will make. It's not about being cocky or egotistical; it's about our self-confidence and feeling good about ourselves and believing in ourselves."

Chapter Nine

The Barking Dogs

J erry sat, thinking for several moments and then asked, "Does anyone have an example of how you have used this power? This ability to bring about positive change?"

"We all have many examples since we use it on an ongoing basis, but Tom has a very interesting story about positive change, if he doesn't mind sharing it," Mary said, looking over at Tom and smiling.

Tom smiled back and said, "No, not at all, although I'm a little embarrassed to talk about it. However, I did make a major breakthrough, and I realized I truly do have free will." He stopped for a moment, considering what to say next, and then continued, "I had had some successes using my personal power, but all of the situations were such that I wasn't really sure. I mean, they all could have happened anyway. I was looking for a change in me that I could say positively was caused by my desire to change, and it had to be something significant, deeply ingrained in me, and difficult to bring about. One day I hit on it.

"For a long time I had been bothered by the dogs in my neighborhood barking. It seems that everyone around me had a dog or dogs that all barked nonstop. It was driving me mad. I would walk outside to enjoy the weather and there it would be, yap, yap, yap, yap, all day, nonstop! It bothered me to the point that I started visiting my neighbors and leaving notes or confronting them about their dogs. I threatened on several occasions to call the county animal control authorities and have them come and take the dog away. In one instance I did contact the county, and they sent a letter to this particular neighbor. Often I would mentally plan how I might do something to the dogs, something like hamburger laced with antifreeze, plans I had no intention of following through with, but they gave me some degree of solace. I felt very justified in my actions and efforts. My neighbors, however, must have thought I was some kind of nut, a raving maniac. Many days I would be totally consumed with the noise; that's all I would think about.

"One evening, my wife and I were sitting outside on our patio having dinner. The dogs had been going at it all day. I was in a semi-foul mood. I wasn't enjoying the meal, although it was a beautiful evening. All I could think about was the noise, that yap, yap, yap. At one point I looked over at my wife and asked her if she could believe the noise those dogs were making. To my surprise she had the audacity to ask, 'What dogs?' I couldn't believe it! Was she deaf? How could she help but hear them? Later, I asked my daughter the same question. The response was the same: 'No, papa, I don't really hear anything. Yeah, there may be dogs barking, but it's just part of the outside noise, like cars and planes. No biggie.' What the heck was going on? Were they barking at some audio wave length and decibel level only I could pick up? This only frustrated me more. When you're on a rampage, it's comforting to have company.

"One day it came to me. I had been practicing self-cultivation for some time, as I mentioned, and I had had some successes. For some reason though, I had totally ignored the barking dog problem. I guess I thought it was real; I felt I was right and justified. But I didn't like myself when I got in these moods, so I decided I wasn't going to let the dogs bother me anymore. If I could stop the dogs, anything was possible. I started by visualizing myself listening to the dogs bark, but instead of being bothered by the barking, I would enjoy it. It was difficult at first; I would go outside and hear the dogs barking, and my internal dialogue would immediately kick in, as it always had before, and start talking negatively about the dogs and the owners and all the things I was going to do that I really wasn't going to do. I realized that the problem was my internal dialogue. That was the culprit! In so many instances it is our enemy. Control your internal dialogue and you will start dictating your life. Why not tell myself something different or at least not think anything? *Ignore* them.

"It took quite some time, about six months or so, but one day I realized I was over the hump. The dogs were not bothering me anymore. Most of the time I didn't even hear them, and when I did, I wasn't bothered. The barking, when I did hear it, had become, instead of an irritant, a reminder of the power I have to bring about positive change, to gradually wipe out those personal characteristics and behaviors in myself I dislike. It corroborated the existence of my free will. In fact, I feel fortunate to have the barking dogs to practice on, otherwise how would I have discovered, conclusively, the personal power I really have? Since then I have had many successes. It is extremely rare that I get angry, depressed, or bothered about much of anything. I see myself differently, and I channel my thoughts in a positive direction. It is amazing the rewards this has brought, and I have barking dogs to thank."

Tom smiled, sat back, and drank the last bit of coffee in his cup. During the silence that followed, Mary said, "Thank you, Tom, for sharing this. We know it's true because he used to rant and rave all the time about the dogs. Is there anything else anyone wants? There's more coffee and mousse."

Jerry said, "What an interesting story, Tom. Thank you. And Mary, if it's not too much trouble, maybe just one more cup of mousse?"

"Me, too," said Jennifer. "I'll go get them. Can I get something for anyone else?"

Looking at her watch, Mary said, "Nothing for me. I'm going to take care of these dishes and go to bed. Tomorrow I need to be at the nursery early."

Tom added, "I need to be going. I have to work early tomorrow also, and my wife should be home by now. She had to work late tonight."

Natalie said, "I need to get to sleep, too. I'll help Mary with the dishes. The two of you can enjoy your mousse."

Jerry got up from the table and gave Mary and Natalie a big hug and shook Tom's hand. "Thanks so much for inviting me tonight,

Mary! And Tom and Natalie, it was a pleasure meeting you, and I'm indebted for what you have shared with me. Thanks so much, all of you, for believing me to be worthy of the apprenticeship. I hope to see you again soon."

"I'm sure you will," said Natalie.

Mary, Tom, and Natalie said goodnight and cleared away the dishes. Jennifer went to get the mousse. When she returned, she sat the mousse cups down and took her seat.

"What a beautiful night," Jerry said. "What fantastic people! You are very fortunate to live here, Jennifer, and work at The Green Patch, and have them as friends."

"You're right," said Jennifer. "Ever since I started taking responsibility and viewing my life in terms of positive possibilities, things have just fallen into place. Not that everything always goes perfectly, but, just like Tom, I sincerely believe that there is little that can happen that I won't know how to deal with. The future has become a place that abounds with possibilities."

"Yes," Jerry said, looking down at his hands. "I guess I have a lot to learn. I am ashamed of my past behavior."

"There is never any reason to regret the past, Jerry. It should be looked at as a learning experience. Try as we may, we can't change what has happened. So many people I see live in the past most of the time. They think the past has a hold on them, but it is only part of the negative feedback, the 'I can't because I was blank this or blank that.' The only thing that matters is right now, this minute, and how we view the future. There is something I want to share with you, Jerry."

Jerry bashfully looked at Jennifer, wondering what she was thinking.

Jennifer continued, "I was watching you tonight and I was very impressed by how fast you picked up on what we were saying. I could sense from your expressions and your body language that you understood. In this way you're just like Mary. Natalie says that she caught on immediately too. It took a while for my thick head to adopt this mind-set. The hard part with many people is achieving the mind-set, the belief, modifying their mental models of the world, changing their paradigms, and I sense you're getting it."

"Thanks, Jennifer. Your impressions mean a lot. Yes, I think I understand. The conversation this evening has been like waking up from a bad dream. All kinds of possibilities are running through my head, whereas before I thought I had none. As I mentioned, I have a presentation on one of my largest projects next week. I will be reviewing it with the site manager and his staff, something I have never done. I know the material, but I have always hated these dog and pony shows, and this will be first time I have made a presentation to Joe Blackburn. Besides, there are some unusual circumstances with this project, so I had been dreading it. But sitting here listening to the four of you tonight, I decided to look at it differently, to look at it as an opportunity to not only show them what I know but to practice this 'mind doesn't know the difference' stuff. Now I can hardly wait!"

"Great, Jerry. I wish you luck. By the way, how is your garden doing?"

"One heck of a lot better than the one last year," Jerry said, laughing. "And since I quit trying to drown my plants with love, it looks like they're recovering. It's funny. Last year I didn't water my garden at all and everything died. This year I was watering too much and nearly killed everything. But it has been a great lesson and I think I'm in tune now, not only to my garden, but to myself. You'll have to come by and see it. I'd appreciate your expert advice and maybe some more little jewels on how to grow my 'tomato brain'. "

"Would love to," said Jennifer, excitedly. "I'm off next Saturday. Maybe I could stop by in the afternoon."

"That would be great. I better get going. It's getting late," said Jerry.

Jennifer walked him to his car. Jerry turned to her and said, "Thanks, again, for tonight, Jennifer. You don't know how much this means to me." He gave her a big hug and waved goodbye. As Jennifer watched the car fade off down the driveway, she smiled to herself.

Chapter Ten

A Change of Mind-set

J erry had such a myriad of thoughts coursing through his head
that he had a hard time going to sleep. Eventually he dropped
of, awaking Sunday morning bright and early. Although he had
gone to bed late, he felt refreshed and wide awake. He vaguely
remembered dreaming about flying. He was in some kind of plane
without wings, but it wasn't scary; it was invigorating. He jumped
out of bed and put on the coffee. After making a large cup of latte,
he walked outside, cup in hand, to check his garden.

All the plants had grown considerably since he looked at them
last, and the new growth was green, not brown. Little flowers
on the tomato plants had begun to form small green tomatoes.
Wonder when the brain starts to develop, he thought, smiling and
recalling the conversation the previous evening. Although the idea
of a "thinking" tomato had seemed ridiculous when Jennifer first
mentioned it, it really was a dramatic analogy. Even low forms
of life, if they had a brain and could act, would take care of their
basic needs. Certainly these poor tomato plants would get water,
nutrients, access to sunlight, or whatever they needed if they were
able to think and move about. Why, then, were so many humans
caught in the victim mentality, acting like vegetables and too often
complaining about their condition rather than doing something
about it?

He thought about his father, whom he respected a great deal for
his solid work ethic and many noble characteristics but had worked
his whole life in a job he seemed to hate. He could still remember

him coming home, exhausted, complaining about the company, his boss, and very often his coworkers. It was always, "They won't let me" or "I can't" or "Someday I'm going to get fed up and quit," but he never did. He just stuck it out and finally retired. The "victim blues" were there after he retired. He always said he was going to travel, start a new business, and remodel the house, but he only sat around, watching sports or staring off into space. On rare occasions he would play golf with his cronies. His father had instilled a respect for authority in Jerry. Position power ruled all. But while he had respect for the positions, he never seemed to have respect for the people in the positions. Jerry realized how grossly inconsistent this was. He could still hear his father saying, "The reason they call it work is because we don't like it. If it was fun, it wouldn't be called work. The only reason for working is to get money. That's how they are able to keep us chained down. We don't have a chance." Two years ago his father had passed away, or maybe he had just faded away from a lack of interest in life.

The negative lesson his father had shown by his dislike of work and his fatalistic outlook was one reason Jerry had decided to pursue electrical engineering. He had loved tinkering around with old radios, TVs, and other electrical gadgets when he was a kid. One positive lesson he could thank his father for: good grades were something expected of him. Jerry had done extremely well in school, graduating at the top of his class at the University of California, Berkeley and landing a job at Microprojects right away. And the first few years went very well. He had been young and naïve back then, not knowing what to expect those first few years. He blamed the transition on the new management style Joe Blackburn brought to the company when he took over as site manager. Jerry realized, though, that he had been acting like his father. When he recalled some recent conversations, he realized he sounded just like him. Was he propagating some genetic victimization trait that had been handed down through the Artson's DNA from generation to generation? Well, this was the new Jerry now. It was time to break the curse. The conversations he had had with Mary, Natalie, Tom, and Jennifer had ignited a belief in self. He was charged with an energy he had not felt for a long time.

Jerry checked the soil for moisture. Half an inch down it was still moist. No need to water again now. No need to drown his plants in love. He stepped back and looked at his garden. It was coming along nicely. There was a parallel here; his garden and he were moving along a similar path of development, except that he had a brain.

Jerry went inside and opened his briefcase, something he brought home often but rarely opened. It seemed like he felt some odd sense of accomplishment by just bringing it home. He pulled out the notes he would be using for the presentation next week. It was on a project he had completed a month ago. It was one of the largest Jerry had handled and was for the installation of a computer control system for the Felton Corporation. There was, however, some controversy over the way the project had been handled. The cost of the job had overrun by twelve percent, but the CEO of Felton had been so pleased with the installation that he had committed to contract Microprojects to do similar projects in five other Felton operations.

Jerry recalled his meeting with Mills to review the costs. Jerry felt that the extra costs were merited in order to provide the product quality their customer deserved, but he failed to convince Mills whose focus seemed to always be the bottom-line costs. Jerry had done something very stupid: he had gone ahead with the more expensive components against Mills's instructions. Feeling like he was between a rock and a hard place, he didn't know how to approach his boss, but he just couldn't give Felton sub-quality components. When Andy found out what happened, he had been livid! Jerry thought he was going to be fired. Mills quickly changed his tune when Felton's CEO committed to five other sites. But Jerry didn't know how to handle the cost-overrun question during the presentation. This was the first one he would make to Joe Blackburn, and he wanted it to go well. In fact, Jerry had met Joe only once, and that was only a brief handshake intro when Joe first arrived. He had passed him in the hall several times, and Joe was always friendly and said hello. Despite this front of friendliness, Jerry had heard a lot of negative feedback from his peers about Joe. Was he really a butcher, like people said, acting now like the wolf in sheep's clothing?

The fact that this was Jerry's first presentation to management combined with the delicate issues involved in this project had caused

Jerry to dread the event. Until last night, he had been considering calling in sick; Mills would have to give the presentation himself. But now his tomato brain was leading him down a different path.

Jerry spent the rest of the day reviewing the data on the project and putting together the PowerPoint material for the presentation. He committed to stick to the facts but decided to leave out the part where Mills had objected to the better components. What would be the point in making him look bad? He had, after all, offered Jerry good advice on several parts of the projects, and he must admit that technically Andy was very sharp. As Jerry completed a slide, he tried to visualize himself standing before Blackburn and his staff, reviewing the information. He imagined what questions he might be asked, and he saw himself answering them with confidence and conviction. He recalled what Jennifer had said, "When we combine practice and pre-work, knowing what we are doing, with a vision of ourselves' succeeding, we greatly increase the probability we will succeed." Jerry also recalled what he had learned about making presentations: speak distinctly, don't rush, say briefly what you will say, say it, then briefly review what you have said, make your presentation simple, make sure you have good eye contact with your audience, but don't hold the contact with any one person more than five seconds, don't turn your back on your audience, and listen intently to their comments—observe—and their questions. And, most important, relax and enjoy it.

Jerry worked all afternoon and then went out and grabbed a bite to eat. After dinner, he picked up the novel he had been trying to read. He felt relaxed. His presentation was Tuesday morning. He could hardly believe he was actually looking forward to it. As he lay in bed reading the novel, the plot of the story mixed with his dreams as he dropped off to sleep.

Chapter Eleven

Jerry Gets a Little "Help" from His Friend

J erry awoke Monday morning earlier than usual. His alarm was set for 6:00, just enough time to shower, dress, and be at work by 7:30. Since he was wide awake, he decided to do something he hadn't done for a long time: exercise. Actually it wasn't exercise as much as it was stretching. He used to get up early every morning and get on the floor, first thing, and do forty-five minutes of yoga stretching. He would finish by doing as many push-ups as he could. Yoga had been a relaxing, slow way to start the day by gradually waking up, but he disliked the push-ups. Over time, he quit getting up early. He dreaded going to work so much that the extra hour of postponing the inevitable overrode any desire to exercise. He looked down at the roll of fat that had accumulated along his midsection. *Ugh,* he thought. *How could I have ever let myself get into such lousy shape?* He rolled out of bed and got on the floor to do his yoga routine. That went well, but he huffed and puffed to do thirty push-ups when he used to be able to do one hundred with little effort. *Oh well*, he thought. *At least it's a start.*

Jerry arrived at work with a spring in his step. He gave everyone he saw a bright "Good morning." Some stared back in disbelief. In his office he checked his e-mail and answered several messages. Gene Larson, one of the engineers Jerry worked with, stuck his head in Jerry's door at 8:30 and asked, "Want to grab a cup of coffee at the cafeteria, Jer?"

"Sure! Why not?" responded Jerry.

As they walked toward the cafeteria, Gene asked Jerry, "How'd your weekend go? We missed you at the bar."

"Believe it or not," Jerry said. "It was one of the best weekends I have had in a long time. I thought about giving you a call, but I was invited to dinner at Mary Green's. She's the owner of The Green Patch Nursery. I met some people who work with her."

They arrived at the cafeteria, purchased their coffee, and sat down.

"The big presentation is tomorrow, huh, Jer?" said Gene with a sly snicker. "I'm glad I'm not in your shoes. You want me to stand by outside the conference room with medical help? You'll most likely need it. That's if you make it through alive!"

"Actually, I'm looking forward to it, Gene," said Jerry with a slight smile. Gene's grin turned into a frown. "No, seriously. I believe I'm going to do well."

"You've got to be kidding, Jer!" said Gene, unbelievingly. "What, with Mills the Maniac in there? He's going to eat you for lunch right in front of the big honchos. It'll be brutal. You know I'm right! You'll see!"

"Yeah, Mills is . . ." then Jerry caught himself. *Speak ill of no one.* " . . . is not so bad," he finished. "He's probably wishing he had given me other advice. I'm going to try and make it come out well for Mills and myself."

"You're what?" Gene shouted. "Hello, Jer? Is that you inside there, ol' buddy?" Gene asked, clowning around, looking at Jerry up close. "What'd you put in that coffee?" he asked, smelling Jerry's coffee. "You know we're not supposed to have alcohol at work."

"It's only the rot-gut cafeteria coffee," Jerry said. "Please don't laugh; I'm serious about the presentation."

"Well, better thee than me, " Gene said, shaking his head in disbelief. "We'd better get back to the grind before big brother finds we've been gone too long."

Chapter Twelve

The Big Presentation

Jerry arrived at work on Tuesday a half hour early. He wanted to make sure he had time to review his notes and slides one last time before his 10:00 presentation. As he opened the door to his office, he noticed a black wreath hanging from his computer screen. *Gene Larson, more than likely,* Jerry thought. At a quarter to eight, Larson and some of the other engineers came by wearing black armbands and snickering like little kids.

"We just came by to wish you good luck," said Gene as they all laughed. "Remember, there's a phone in Blackburn's conference room. You can call nine-one-one anytime."

"Nothing like the strong support of your comrades when you are going into battle," said Jerry, laughing with an air of confidence that surprised the whole group.

"We promise we'll all be pallbearers," said Gene.

"Thanks a lot. Now please go play somewhere else," he said with good humor. "I still have some work to do before this thing starts."

Jerry arrived at the conference room at 9:50. Anita Evans, Blackburn's administrative assistant, looked bored to tears. She greeted Jerry as he walked up, saying with a tinge of sympathy, "You're on next, but Fred Billings is still in there. Have a seat and I'll call you when they're ready."

Jerry sat down where he had a good view of the conference room door and the clock. He practiced breathing slowly and turning off his internal dialogue. The clock ticked past 10:00, each minute sounding like the strike of a gong. Finally, at 10:30, the conference room opened and Billings walked out, the blood drained from his worried face, shaking his head and looking grim.

"Whew. I'm glad that's over," he said. "You're on the grill next, Artson. Good luck!"

Jerry walked slowly over to the door. For a moment he felt like he was going to the gallows, but just then he recalled Mary's words: *We just stop doing it. Whenever we catch ourselves feeding ourselves negative thoughts, we will ourselves to think the opposite. All right,* Jerry thought as he opened the door, *this is going to be fun!*

Joe Blackburn was sitting at the end of a long, mahogany conference table. Large, abstract paintings adorned the walls. A tall modern sculpture stood in one corner. An expansive picture window looked out on the manicured lawns of Microprojects' grounds. At the opposite end of the table from Blackburn was a large projection screen. Joe's management staff sat around the table. All had their jackets off, sleeves of white dress shirts rolled up, and ties loose like a bunch of twiddle-dee-dees. As Jerry walked up to the front of the table, Andy Mills, who sat two seats down from the projector, winked and gave him a worried smile. The rest seemed to be checking him out as if he were some new species of beast.

Blackburn said, "Thanks for coming, Jerry. Sorry for making you wait so long. Sometimes this bunch likes to beat a subject to death," he droned, eyeing the staff and shaking his head. "But we're ready for some good news. Please tell us about the Felton Project."

Jerry thanked Joe and his staff for the opportunity to talk to them. He plugged in his flash drive with the PowerPoint information and jumped into his presentation. He felt all the anxiety he had been feeling turn to energy. He sensed a rush of adrenaline, but at the same time he was relaxed. He covered the material as planned, pausing periodically for questions about the specifics of how the project had been done. All of the questions he had correctly anticipated in his pre-work. When he got to the part about the project overrun, he caught Andy's eye and saw him wince. Jerry continued his presentation, supporting the cost overrun with a slide listing the benefits of the more-expensive components. The next slide illustrated why these benefits had been a major factor in Felton's CEO's favorable reaction and his decision to duplicate this system at five other Felton sites. Jerry gazed over at Andy, whose face had gone white. Looking at Andy, he told the group how much he appreciated his boss's support throughout the project. He said that without his advice it would probably not have been successful. Jerry realized that this was a little twist of the truth, but Andy had been helpful through most of the project. There was no reason to make Mills look bad. *He might as well take this opportunity to sweeten up some of the flowers in his relationship with Mills,* he thought.

When he finished, he knew he had done well. Blackburn, who had said nothing during the entire presentation, sat smiling at him and nodding his head slowly. Then, amazing everyone, he stood and said that Jerry deserved a round of applause. All joined in, but Mills, with a look on his face like he had just been given clemency from a death sentence, clapped the loudest. Jerry thanked them and walked out of the conference room. As soon as the door closed he loudly shouted "Yes!" Surprised, Anita Evans dropped the teacup she held, and Don Miller, next in line for presentation-ville, almost fell out of his seat. Both looked at Jerry as if he were crazy.

When Jerry arrived back at his office, Gene and two other engineers were waiting for him. They expected to see Jerry's typical long face and goad him on as he relived the horrors of the presentation. It would also be an opportunity to do some major character bashing of Blackburn and his staff. Jerry was a real wit when it came to painting distorted caricatures of people. Instead, Jerry walked in, smiling ear to ear as if he had just won the lottery.

"So, how'd it go, Jer?" asked Gene, a little disappointed at Jerry's composure.

"Fantastic," Jerry said. "Just like I imagined it would be."

"So what happened?" asked Gene, marveling that he had escaped the lion's den.

"I just told them the truth," said Jerry. "Well, *almost* the truth."

"Old Maniac Mills must be hating you now, huh Jer?" asked Gene, hoping he could salvage some tidbit of destruction from the story.

"No, it was a great opportunity to improve my relationship with Mills," said Jerry. "I think we both came out smelling like roses."

"Oh," said Gene, "I see," although he was actually totally confused.

"Well guys, I need to get caught up on my e-mail. Why don't we do lunch later and I'll tell you what went on," said Jerry, walking over to his computer.

"Sure," mumbled Gene and the other engineers. "See you later."

At lunch, Jerry told the group what had happened. They all sat in wonder as he related the particulars of the meeting.

Joe Blackburn was sitting in his office thinking about the presentation Jerry had made. Periodically Joe asked employees, picked more or less at random, to come in and talk to him about how the company was doing, if they liked their jobs, what could be improved for the company and the individual, and so on. Joe had been concerned for some time about the direction the culture of the organization was headed. Overall, he didn't like what he was hearing from the employees. The previous division manager had been strong in command and control. Joe realized the downsizing had taken a toll. He was contemplating ways to reverse the damage because he knew that employee morale had a tremendous impact on company performance. This guy Jerry Artson seemed to have his head in the right place. He suspected Andy Mills might be difficult to have as a boss, as he did of some of the other managers, and he had been trying to coach Mills and the rest in better leadership skills. In spite of potential difficulties working with Mills, Jerry had handled the project well. Joe suspected Jerry had shaded the truth a little as he described how he *and Mills* decided on the cost overrun, but that only caused him to respect Jerry more. Joe was impressed by Jerry's delivery style and how he handled the questions from his staff. Maybe Jerry could provide some additional insight into ways the culture could be impacted. Joe had always had an uncanny ability to read people, and he possessed an exceptional intuitive ability. He decided to ask Jerry to stop by soon so he could discuss it with him and get his perspective. It couldn't hurt.

After lunch, Jerry was sitting in his office reading some mail when the phone rang. "Hello, Jerry Artson speaking," he said.

"Jerry, this is Joe Blackburn. I just wanted to thank you for the great presentation you made this morning. I wonder if you have time to stop by my office on Thursday, say about 10:00. I want to talk to you about some things."

"Sure, Mr. Blackburn. No problem. I'll make time."

"Good," said Blackburn. "See you then. And, by the way, please call me Joe."

After Jerry hung up, the familiar cloud of doom floated by as he thought, *I wonder what I've done now?* Then he caught himself. *Hey, I just gave the best presentation of my career to the head man. He probably wants to talk about that. And if he doesn't, I can deal with whatever he does want to discuss.* The cloud of doom parted, and bright shiny thoughts replaced the gloom.

Chapter Thirteen

Jerry Meets with Joe Blackburn

*T*hursday rolled around quickly, and Jerry found himself standing outside Joe Blackburn's door. He had used his imagination to paint a vision of Joe and himself carrying on an open dialogue about some topic or other. He had also brushed up on the details of all of his recent projects, just in case Joe wanted to discuss any of them. He looked forward to the encounter. After all, this was the first time he had ever been in Joe's office. Opportunities like this didn't come around very often.

Jerry tapped on Joe's door at the designated time and, after a few seconds, Joe opened the door and extended his hand. "Come in, Jerry. Thank you for meeting with me on such a short notice."

Jerry looked around Joe's office. It was larger than Mills's, but not as ostentatious. It had a tasteful business decor. Several stacks of paper and folders were strewn around his desk. Joe directed Jerry to sit on a couch by the window while Joe sat in an adjacent chair. This was more relaxed and had less of a boss–subordinate feeling than Andy's office.

"I want to express again how impressed we were with your presentation the other day, Jerry," Joe began. "This Felton deal is going to be one of our most profitable contracts. The initiative and foresight you and Andy took to upgrade the components for Felton showed great management skill. Budgets are, after all, only an estimate. Some come in low, some high. Although we might have a problem if all of them were overruns, the important thing is that we look after our customers, make the right decisions, and learn from our mistakes. You wouldn't believe some of the boondoggles I made in my younger days, but I consider them learning experiences," he laughed. Then more seriously he said, "But this isn't why I asked you to stop by, Jerry. I have something else I want to discuss with you."

"What is that, sir?" Jerry asked, sounding a little worried.

"Well, Jerry, you are aware that this division has gone through some significant downsizing or right sizing or whatever you want to call it. I was given the job of cutting out the fat in the organization, which I have done. Unfortunately, it has left some deep scars. I fear that we may have lowered the trust level farther than the headcount. Eliminating middle-management positions and superfluous jobs will create a lot of short-term bottom-line black ink, but I'm afraid the way we went about it may eventually turn the black ink to red if we don't act quickly to regain our employees' trust. I have a goal to empower the organization by reducing the need for so many levels of management and shift the responsibility to the people actually doing the work. I can tell that too often the culture here is a check-with-your-boss-before-you-act culture, and I don't believe that this is healthy for the long-term success of the company. If we could bring it about, Microprojects would not only be a great company but a terrific place to work. I want to empower the people who interact directly with our customers. Working through my staff, this is what we have been trying to achieve, but I fear it's not working. People don't seem to care, and there's a lack of pride of ownership and team solidarity. I suspect that our employees spend a lot of time complaining about the company, which is a waste of time, not to mention the impact this has on their work ethic and attitude.

"I've been sort of randomly asking employees like you how they like working here, and if they have any suggestions for improvement. I must admit that even though I have been here for almost a year, I haven't given anyone but my immediate staff the opportunity to know me. I was extremely busy with some company legal issues after I came on board a year ago, but I think we have those under control at last. I am scheduling meetings like this with a cross section of employees. One of my top priorities is to give everyone a better idea of who I am, where I'm coming from, my vision for the company, and most important, hear their concerns. I was excited by your presentation the other day. For one thing we haven't had much good news lately, but the other part is that I was impressed by your delivery and how you handled yourself. So I thought, why not ask this guy in and see what he thinks."

Jerry took a long pause. He wasn't sure how open he should be with Joe. Based on the rumors he had heard about him, *some of which Jerry had spread himself*, he should be cautious. But the man didn't seem to resemble any of the stories; in fact, he appeared to be just the opposite. His comments about the company seemed to indicate he did care. Jerry decided to go with his gut feel; the ability to judge people was, after all, one of the characteristics he had written on his list of personal power attributes.

"To be honest, sir, I haven't enjoyed working here as of late. It seems like, even during the command-and-control era, it was a better place to work. I like the work, I like our customers, but I think there's way too much red tape associated with everything we do. Often it is very frustrating, and sometimes I feel like giving up or looking for a job elsewhere."

Joe gazed at Jerry a few seconds, which momentarily caused Jerry to worry that he had been too honest. But Joe's demeanor, to the contrary, indicated openness. Finally he asked, "Do you have any insights as to the root of the problem and what can be done to turn it around? I sincerely want to empower the employees in order to get rid of a lot of the red tape you refer to."

"Two things must happen for empowerment to take place, sir," Jerry said, recalling what Mary had said, and choosing his words carefully. "Those at the top of the organizational pyramid must give up power, and those at the bottom of the pyramid, the people who do most of the work, must accept or even take power. As I am sure you are aware, this is called turning the organization upside-down. It is only natural that managers are hesitant to relinquish or share power. But since power, in addition to being let go, must be in turn taken by those at the bottom of the pyramid, a significant problem lies with them. They must take responsibility, be proactive, and be in control of their own destinies. The foundation of an empowered workforce is built on individuals who take responsibility. Unless this transformation occurs, nothing will change, at least nothing enduring. One significant reason is that even the best organizations neglect the needs of their people at least some of the time. Not intentionally, but because organizations consist of fallible human beings. Besides, managers should have more important things to do than babysit their employees all the time. One of the biggest problems with most organizations and society, in general, is not a lack of leadership but a lack of willingness on the part of ordinary people to take responsibility."

Blackburn sat back in his chair, looking at Jerry with even more respect than before. After contemplating what Jerry had said, he asked, "And what is the answer, Jerry? How does this magical transformation occur?"

"Something called organizational gardening and self-cultivation, sir. I know these names sound a little hokey," Jerry said, almost regretting he had even mentioned them, "but it's about creating the right environment for people to excel *and* develop on their own. It's about providing for their needs, but more important, teaching them how to fulfill their own needs. And it's about treating people like natural beings, not inanimate machines."

"This is quite profound, Jerry. Where did you learn about these organizational gardening and self-cultivation theories?" Joe asked with keen interest.

"Where else, sir?" Jerry said, trying not to sound flippant. "From the people who work at a large nursery in the city."

"They must be very special people," Joe replied.

Jerry said, "They are, sir. The owner, Mary Green, has been a friend of my mother's for years. I see her from time to time, but I visited her recently after not seeing her for a long period. As I mentioned, sir, I was feeling down about my job and had gone there to see her and get my mind off work and maybe buy some plants to start a garden. I feel I should apologize for saying this about work, but it's the truth. Somehow, I feel I can be honest with you. Anyway Mary slowly introduced me to a variety of concepts, ideas I had never thought about before. Then she decided to take me on as an apprentice, an apprentice of ideas, concepts, possibilities concerning self-reliance or self-leadership; what she calls self-cultivation. My only obligation is to practice what I have learned. I still don't understand why she picked me, but since she and some of the other people who work there have been sharing their ideas with me, my life has improved in many ways, including my work life. I've come to realize that I am the cause of most of my problems simply by how I look at things. The way my presentation came across the other day had a lot to do with Mary."

Joe sat silently, looking at Jerry and slowly nodding, and then he said, "What you say is interesting, Jerry, very interesting indeed."

Joe canceled his next meeting, and they discussed organizational gardening and self-cultivation until about noon. Jerry didn't mention the thinking tomato. He wasn't sure whether Joe was ready for this analogy or not. *Now there's even a greater need to learn more about Mary's concepts,* he thought.

Friday afternoon, Jerry was sitting in his office when Gene stuck his head in the door. *What now?* Jerry thought.

"Hey, Jer. How goes it?"

"Great, Gene," Jerry responded. "What's up?"

"Say, Jer," Gene asked a little hesitantly. "I have a presentation to do in about two weeks, and I was wondering if you would share some of your pointers with me. Maybe give me some, uh, well . . . you know, some coaching."

"No problem, Gene," Jerry said. "Be glad to." *And I'll be increasing my personal power,* he thought to himself.

Chapter Fourteen

The Power of Vision

On Friday, for the first time in years, Jerry hated to leave work. But he was looking forward to seeing Jennifer on Saturday and getting some pointers on his garden and organizational gardening. He got up early to go to the market to buy fresh vegetables and some fish in case Jennifer stayed for dinner. Jerry prided himself on being a good cook. *Wonder if that should go on my personal power list?* he asked himself. He put a nice bottle of champagne in the refrigerator. This past week was definitely a cause for celebration. He also straightened up his house; no point in appearing to live like a pig.

Jennifer arrived mid afternoon. Jerry was glad to hear her voice on the phone and nearly started telling her about the past week when she asked him how he was doing. Instead, he just said "great," deciding to wait until he saw her in person to share the details. When the doorbell rang, Jerry hurried to greet her. She looked great in a pair of khaki shorts, a colorful tee shirt that said "LA Marathon" on the back, and white tennis shoes.

"Hello, Jennifer," Jerry said, opening the door.

"Hi, Jerry. Hope I'm not late."

Jerry showed Jennifer his house. Although he didn't have a lot of furniture, the place was tastefully decorated, and Jennifer was impressed. He took her outside and showed her his vegetable garden. Jerry wondered what she was thinking as she silently inspected the plants.

"It looks great. The only thing I might recommend is adding some stakes to support the tomatoes and beans. Otherwise they will run along the ground. Then either the bugs get them or the tomatoes drop to the ground and rot. This is how they have evolved to propagate. As you probably know, the tomato fruit carries the seeds and provides nourishment and proper acidity as it decomposes while the seeds take root in the soil."

"Thanks," Jerry said, laughing. "So a thinking tomato would probably take itself down from the stakes so it could properly propagate."

"I guess it might," Jennifer said, smiling. "Speaking of thinking tomatoes, how did your week go? How was your big presentation you were so worried about?"

"I could hardly wait for you to ask," Jerry said excitedly. "My fear gradually abated as I practiced what all of you taught me last weekend. Has it been only a week since our dinner at Mary's? So much has happened since then; it seems like a long time ago."

Jerry described his week to Jennifer, including the preparation on Sunday, the comments by Gene and the engineers, the presentation to Blackburn and his staff, and his subsequent meeting with Blackburn and his interest in transforming Microprojects' culture. He even mentioned the "coaching" request he received from Gene on making better presentations. Jerry described all of this with such delight and energy that he reminded Jennifer of a young child telling of a first visit to the zoo. She sat quietly and listened until he had finished.

"All of us felt you would pick this up quickly," she said when he had finally finished. "But we had no idea you would become a transition figure so soon."

"Yeah, thanks to all of you," Jerry said with sincerity. "I had good teachers. But now I am anxious to find out more. First and foremost, I want to know for myself. But I think Blackburn is going to want to know more, too. I would like to be able to fill him in on the next chapter if that occasion arises."

"Just-in-time learning," Jennifer laughed. "OK. Are you ready for lesson number two? Or is it three?"

"I'm ready," he said. "I think it's lesson four. Why don't we sit over there in the shade of that oak tree?"

They walked over to an area under a large oak where Jerry had earlier placed some chairs and a table. Jennifer began, "The second lesson of self-cultivation is about something called *vision*. It's that subcategory of our imagination we discussed earlier."

"You mean the one that our subconscious can't differentiate from reality?" laughed Jerry.

"Absolutely," said Jennifer. "But vision is out there in the future. It is a mental picture of how we would want our lives to look if everything was going right. It could be anything, but preferably there's a lot of emotion tied to these mental images of the future, the kind that get us excited, that make us want to go there. It could be about wealth or health or success or accomplishment or knowledge or winning or breaking a bad habit or whatever. It depends because it is very individual, very personal. No one can tell us what our vision is. We can tie it to our major roles in life or to the way we wish to create a legacy. We first create the mental picture, and then we may want to write it down on paper. Some people do, some don't. We call it a *vision statement*. I think about mine so often that there is no need to have it written anymore, although initially I had a copy on my wall.

"Once we have a clear image of our future desired state, we focus on the present situation: the way it is today, what we want to change. We call it our *current reality*. The more honest we are with ourselves, the clearer the picture of our current reality becomes. Often, our focus on the present helps us create our image of the future. The more we think about the way it is today compared to the way we want it to be, the more desire we generate for change. We produce a true commitment, similar to the motivation we create when we focus on our personal power. But our vision is directional, that is, it gives us the impetus to move toward a specific picture we want to emulate in the future. The more we think about it, the more energy we create. This energy becomes motivation that translates into actions, specific actions that move us closer to achieving our vision. At some point we find our lives are changing. The unwanted present dissolves into the past, and we begin to realize our dreams. This fuels a greater desire to mentally describe the future more distinctly, which again fuels our desire for change. It is all very powerful; visioning is perhaps the most powerful tool we possess. It is all built on taking responsibility for creating the world we want."

"Wow!" Jerry said after a moment. "Can you give me an example of something you have envisioned? Something you have changed in yourself?"

"Sure, I can share an example that's easy to understand but was very hard for me to do," she said, gazing at a squirrel scampering along a branch high in the oak. "Five years ago, when I first came to work at the nursery, I was a lot heavier. In fact, I have to say I was downright fat. I didn't like myself. I hated to look in the mirror. I hated to buy clothes because I felt like I was shopping for a tent. I would look at Mary Green and envy her physique. Here was this older lady who didn't look old, who had a kind of ethereal beauty. She wasn't arrogant or vain about it; it was just the way she was. I sensed there was no other option for her. I had always made excuses for myself; there was always some reason or other why I was perfectly justified to sit around on my fat butt. I think a lot of it stemmed from my childhood. I was chubby as a kid, perhaps because I am the youngest of three, and they all spoiled me by feeding me. My two older brothers kidded me a lot about my weight. I don't believe they realized the impact it had on me. My self-esteem was damaged, and it affected many other aspects of my life as well."

"I would never have guessed," Jerry said seriously.

"Probably not, but I was a different person back then in more ways than one. When I applied for work at the nursery, Mary may have intuitively felt that I had potential, or she may have felt sorry for me, or, more likely, that is just the way she treats everyone. Then I learned about observation, responsibility, choice, imagination, and the power of vision, so I vowed to change. I decided my first priorities would be my health, my physical well-being, and my appearance. It would be a good way to try this stuff out, to see if it worked. I nearly made a big mistake, though, taking on something that major. One should start with something a little easier. Failure on the first endeavor might sour one on the whole concept. But I was fortunate because I had Mary and Natalie's help. I started by visualizing myself shopping for a size eight or nine dress, proudly wearing a bikini, and running a long distance without being exhausted. It wasn't easy at first; in fact, it was downright hard. Often during the first few months I would cry myself to sleep because I was so discouraged. But only because I reverted to my old habit of feeding myself a lot of negative stuff, just like I used to stuff myself with a ton of sweets. Gradually I was able to keep my vision intact and successfully banish the negative thoughts. I focused on my personal power. I sought help from Mary and Natalie when I couldn't find the support within. Slowly, over time, it became easier and easier, and one day I looked in the mirror and I realized I had changed. I actually looked good. Today it's not so much a part of my vision as it is my normal routine. Being fit and healthy is a part of my current reality that I love, and I wouldn't trade them for the world. The positive habit has become learned. That's what visioning is about, Jerry. It's the stuff that transforms people, organizations, societies, whole nations."

Jerry looked at Jennifer's slender, muscular arms and legs and her small waist and said, "I can't believe you were ever overweight, much less fat or obese, but I have to believe you. No one could describe something with such conviction otherwise."

"Believe me, I was. I'm not telling you this to brag about my accomplishments or to make you think 'Oh, my' about my physique. I don't have anything against people who are overweight. For me, though, my weight was a big deal. I tell you about it because it is my best example of the power of commitment and change that a compelling vision creates. Here . . . take a look at this picture," Jennifer said, pulling a photograph of herself out of her purse.

"Wow," Jerry exclaimed. "This can't be you."

"Well, it is. Then again, it isn't. It's not only my appearance that's different. It's what was in my head back then, too. Neither resembles the 'Jennifer' of today."

Jerry recalled his vision of the roll of fat around his midsection as he lay in bed the other morning. "Yeah, I need some of that myself. I used to be in really good shape, but I quit exercising when my work life went south. I blamed it on that, but it was just another excuse. Now that I realize that I haven't been taking responsibility for one of my most basic needs, my health and physical well-being. It's pretty pathetic, huh? But I'm committed to change, particularly when I see the example you've set. Any other hints as to how I can accomplish such a transformation?"

"Yes, Jerry. I can share a couple of ideas or concepts with you that might be of help," Jennifer said as she placed the photo back in her purse and pulled out pen and paper. "The first is called the pyramid of learning, or sometimes it is called the ladder or pyramid of change. It was developed by a man named Robert Dilts and based on work by Gregory Bateson. The second part comes from Mary and is based on a unique aspect of self-cultivation called the Seven P's. You might remember us referring to them the other night at Mary's."

"Yes, I recall. What do the P's stand for?" Jerry asked.

"First, let me describe the learning pyramid, Jerry, because there is a strong connection between the two."

Jennifer drew a pyramid on the sheet of paper, made four horizontal lines across it, and wrote *environment* at the bottom. "All learning and all change are about creating a different environment," Jennifer explained. "Environment includes all the things in our life: what we do, where we are, how we live, who we interact with, our moods and attitudes, everything. My environment several years ago included a lot of extra pounds. See what I mean?"

"Well, sort of," Jerry said. "Tell me more."

"How do we change our environment?" she asked.

"Uh, I'm not sure, but probably our behavior has the biggest influence on our environment. That and the actions of other people around," Jerry said.

"You're right, Jerry," Jennifer said, writing *behavior* in the second level of the pyramid. "But for now, we are just talking about us as individuals, how we alone can impact our environment. Now what do you think has the biggest impact on our behavior?"

Jerry thought and said, "I'm not sure, but probably the way we are brought up—our parents, teachers, and friends."

"Yes, those have an affect on our behavior, but there is something more direct. It's called our *ability,*" she said, writing the word in the third level of the pyramid. "Our ability covers everything we know how to do. We can't behave in a specific way if we don't know how. It's about our knowledge and skills, that is, the 'how to'. "

"OK, if you say so," Jerry responded, sounding a little perplexed.

"Don't worry. This will make more sense after I finish the whole pyramid," Jennifer said. "What most influences our ability? What caused you to go to school and become an electrical engineer?"

"I think I know this one," Jerry said, brightening up. "It's what I mentioned before: the way we are raised, our beliefs and our values. One thing my parents instilled in me was that a formal, advanced education was absolutely necessary. I never felt I had a choice."

"You did have a choice, but in this case you probably made the right one. And you are correct, our beliefs influence our ability," she said as she wrote *beliefs* in the fourth level of the pyramid.

"Now, what is at the top of the drawing? When we focus on this, we ultimately make the greatest impact on our environment. And here's a hint: it's directly related to the transformation I made over the last five years."

Jerry thought for a few moments, and then his face took on an expression that resembled a light bulb being turned on in a dark room. "It's what you said about the way you saw yourself: the bikini, the size-eight dress, completing a marathon. It's about how we see ourselves, isn't it? Our self-image?"

"Exactly, Jerry," Jennifer said, pleased with his insight. "It is called our *identity*" she said as she wrote the word in the top level of the pyramid.

"When we focus on our identity, who we are or how we would like to be, there is a greater likelihood we will change. Recall Tom's 'barking dogs' endeavor. He started making progress when he began seeing himself as one not bothered by a barking noise. It all goes back to the power obtained from planting positive seeds in our subconscious. As we change our identity, we transform our beliefs, and beliefs structure how we see the world. They have a powerful influence on our abilities. As we gain new and different abilities, we are able to modify our behaviors and ultimately our environment. Unfortunately, too many programs in too many organizations are aimed at changing only behavior. That's why so many fail. Without the belief and also the ability, all that is achieved is short-term acting that quickly degrades to the previous behavior once the external force, such as fear or retribution or even reward, is removed."

"Yes, I can identify with that," Jerry said as he recalled Microprojects' futile efforts at empowering the organization. "This kind of parallels with vision doesn't it? Our identity is really our vision of who we want to be, and it must create the most energy for change."

"Absolutely," said Jennifer. "That is why there's such a close parallel with the Seven P's. Vision is about the long term; the pyramid of change can be used to bring about change both long and short term. Long term, it is about who we want to be, how we would like to see ourselves in the future. In the long term, I might see myself as being a star or president of the company. Short term, our comments reveal a lot about how we see ourselves. Statements like 'I've never been very athletic' or 'I always have trouble meeting new people' are really identity statements. We see, we identify with being like this, so there is a greater probability we will be. These are negative identity statements, and it is better to make a positive statement like 'I see myself meeting new people easily' or at least making no statement at all. But, Jerry, it's starting to get a little dark. You mind if we move inside?"

"Any chance you're getting hungry? I have some fresh halibut in the refrigerator I can barbecue. And I took the liberty of chilling a nice bottle of champagne. Does that, along with a fresh salad, appeal to you?"

"Perfectly," Jennifer exclaimed. "I don't know where the afternoon went, but I'm famished!"

Chapter Fifteen

The Seven P's

Jerry prepared the halibut while Jennifer made a salad. Once the meal was ready, Jerry popped the champagne.

"Last week was such a success I think it is worth celebrating," Jerry said. He poured two glasses and proposed a toast. "To self-cultivation."

"To *your* self-cultivation," Jennifer responded as they clicked glasses.

They dug into the fish and were silent as they ate and enjoyed the meal.

"Excellent dinner, Jerry," Jennifer commented. "Where did you learn to cook so well?"

"I enjoy cooking, and I've experimented with various recipes for years, but sometimes I get tired of eating alone," Jerry responded.

"I'm lucky. Mary is an excellent cook, and she always insists on preparing food for Natalie and me. She's become a mother figure to both of us. My parents passed away some years ago, and my two brothers live back east, so I don't have any family here. Mary is as close to family as I can get. I think we may also help fill the void left by the loss of her husband and son."

"That must have been terrible for her," Jerry said. "Let's see now, Benjamin would have been about twenty now, probably just finishing college. Did you know he was a sort of child prodigy? He took after his father, who had a PhD in physics. There was a rumor that John was being considered for the Nobel Prize in physics. It was a terrible loss in many respects, but of course, mostly for Mary. Does she ever talk about it?"

"Only on rare occasions," said Jennifer. "I think she doesn't want to burden us with her past. It's probably incredibly difficult for her to talk about."

The two finished their meal in silence as they thought about Mary and all she had endured. She was an amazing example of human resilience.

Finally, Jerry said, "Do you have time to explain the P's to me, Jennifer?"

"I think so," she said. "It's the least I can do as payment for this great meal!" she continued. "There are seven P's. You know, seven is a magic number, and the seventh P is the most magic of all. She took a sheet of paper and drew a picture of a flower with seven petals. In the center of the flower she wrote *vision*.

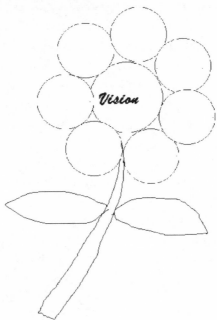

"You recall our conversation at dinner the other night, the description of our personal power?" Jennifer asked.

"Yes, very much so. What I learned has already helped me," Jerry answered.

"You remember that personal power is like the nutrients in the soil. The more power we can tap, the better it will be for us. It is there to be used at any time. The P's, however, emanate from the sun."

"From the sun?" Jerry asked. "How so?"

"Not literally," Jennifer responded, "metaphorically. Vision is to us like the sun is to a plant. The sun's rays provide a catalyst that allows the plant to produce chlorophyll, a process called photosynthesis. Vision provides a catalyst for our subconscious. It draws us to it, and it gives us energy; it motivates us to change, like plants turn to the sun. Our personal power is like the nutrients in the soil. It is there for us to draw on any time so we can use the energy generated by our vision to move toward our vision.

"As we establish a clear and compelling vision of our future, our lives start to take on a purpose." She wrote *purpose* in one of the seven petals. "We begin to know where we are going. We are not just acting at random. We are acting for a reason and with direction. We know what we are about; more essentially, we know what is important to us and what is not. Whatever we are doing revolves around this central purpose, and our beliefs begin to mirror our desired identity. Purpose, then, is the first P, and it emanates from our vision."

"Purpose creates a direction, an excitement, a desire, a motivation, an energy, a passion for moving toward our vision and our new identity.

"It is intrinsically tied to the sometimes elusive 'want to' we've discussed previously. Without a purpose, there is a greater likelihood our 'want to' will ebb and flow depending on what is happening in our life; but purpose causes it to be present at some level all the time. It becomes a safe harbor when our lives hit a storm. It allows us to discard and not worry about the multitude of small, insignificant distractions that can get in our way and have nothing to do with our vision. *Passion* is the second P.

"The next 'P' is *process,* or it could also be called *planning.* Whereas passion provides the 'want to,' processes are about the 'how to'. They allow us to leverage our skills and make a greater impact on achieving our vision. If we choose the right processes, our movement toward our vision is easier. Since difficulty impedes our progress, making it easier increases the probability we will press on. But process without passion is pretty much worthless. There has been a tendency for organizations to focus a lot more on the processes than on people's desire. Unfortunately, or fortunately, depending on how you look at it, if people don't 'want to,' they won't. Yes, you can obtain some semblance of a contribution by driving them with fear, guilt, or temporary reward, but it is only a shadow of what can be achieved with true commitment, and fear and guilt have a way of creating a lot of negative consequences later. Process without passion is like a new car without gas. It may be a brand new Mercedes, for example, the finest of the processes, but without any gas it's going nowhere. Passion is the petrol of processes. For instance, goal setting is an excellent example of a process. It's a powerful tool that helps us move forward, but unless it is done in the context of our greater vision, it may not be worth very much."

The fourth 'P' is pace. This 'P' is about how much energy or effort we put into achieving our vision, how fast we go about it, the rate or speed. This one might surprise you. One might think that the speed would be all out, hell bent, but this is a great misconception and one of the major reasons people fail to achieve their visions. Consider this diagram," Jennifer said as she drew another diagram on the paper:

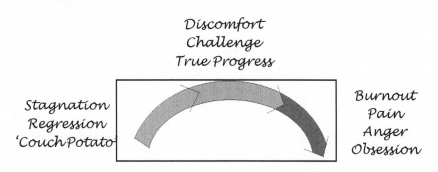

"There are three levels of energy or effort. The first is called stagnation. Nothing is happening here. I call it the 'couch potato' level. In the stagnation level one might be hoping or even praying something will happen but not doing anything. It's the typical mind-set of many people; they hope their lives will change but do nothing to bring about the change. Granted, hope is important; that's what generates the passion, but at some point action is required. If nothing is done for long enough, regression may occur; that is, they begin to lose what they may already have, their muscles may weaken and atrophy, they may grow weaker, they may lose interest, or their knowledge and skills may become obsolete.

"Let's look at the third part of the effort diagram, burnout. Unlike the first level, where there is no effort, at the burnout level there is too much effort. We put so much energy into what we are trying to achieve that we quickly tire of it, or we injure ourselves, or we become angry and obsessive. I recall many times in the past when I decided to diet. I would launch into one of those crash diets hell bent, then grow tired or discouraged after just a few days. Several times I got very sick. One time I had to be hospitalized!

"The middle level of effort, and the only correct pace, is called improvement or true progress. Whereas with the burnout level there is pain, with improvement there is discomfort but no pain. The idea is to start off slowly, like so often happens in nature. When we examine nature we see that long-lasting plants start slowly. One species of Japanese bamboo has almost no growth for the first four years, and then during the fifth year it grows eighty feet! During those first four years it is adjusting, spreading out its root system, building its personal power. The California sequoia, one of the tallest and longest-living things on earth, takes eight years to germinate, eight years! The key is to start slowly and gradually put more energy and effort into what we are doing. The optimum place to be is at the interface of improvement and burnout, but still on the side of improvement. We move up to this point gradually. When we first experience pain or anger, we move back slightly so that we are experiencing discomfort but not pain, challenge but not obsession and anger, progress but not burnout. Make sense?"

"Yes, I think I understand what you are saying, Jennifer," Jerry responded. "Several years ago I decided I would start running. I went out the first day and ran so hard I pulled a muscle. It was very painful; in fact it was painful while I was running, but my macho ego wouldn't let me stop. The next day I could barely walk. It hurt for a long time. Needless to say, I stopped running altogether."

"You're right, Jerry. Sounds like all my futile efforts to lose weight; they all ended in failure until I started applying the Seven P's and finding the right pace. Over time, as we develop both physically and mentally, the interface moves forward, and we are able to accomplish things that would have caused pain, obsession, or burnout previously."

"The fifth P is for *progress*, that is, where we concentrate our focus on our journey to our vision. True progress comes from the right pace. At some point, if we are not making measurable progress, we need to go back and examine our vision to make sure it is not totally unrealistic. We also need to examine the processes we are using to achieve our vision to make sure we can leverage our effort at the current pace. But progress may come slowly, or it may come in spurts. Sometimes we may feel that no progress is being made even when we have a realistic vision and the appropriate processes in place to help us. The important thing is to focus on whatever progress we are making, no matter how small it is, not on how far we have to go. When we focus on our progress, it gives us energy to go on. When we focus only on how far we have to go, we may become discouraged and quit.

"The sixth P stands for the *present*. Have you ever thought about that word? One might think that it has two entirely different meanings. One definition is a gift or 'to give'; the other represents the now, today, or this moment. But of all the gifts we have received, the greatest may be experiencing the *now*. The sixth P is important because often people live too much in the past or the future. They may think too much about what could have been. We think, 'If I had only done this or that, then life would be so different.' But try as we may, it is impossible to go back into the past. What has happened has happened. Not that we can't learn from the past, but there is a vast difference between living in the past and learning from the past. Our vision is in the future, and it is important to experience what it will be like by mentally seeing ourselves there. But remember, nothing happens in the future; it all happens in the now, in the present. We get our energy and our passion from the vision of the future. We learn from the past, but all of the doing, the stuff that creates change, takes place in the present.

"I'm not sure how to say this." She paused as she took another sip of champagne, her voice taking on a slight emotion. "But the seventh 'P' may be the most important of all," she said as she added the seventh P, completing the flower.

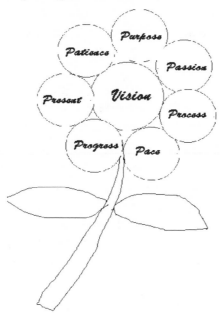

"It's *patience,* and it's perhaps the greatest of all virtues. Purpose is of course very important, as is passion, and the two will probably create the processes one way or the other. But patience is different stuff. It can be the hardest to learn. No matter how much of the first six P's we have, they will probably die on the vine without patience. Too much passion can be the enemy of patience because we get so revved up and excited, particularly when we have created a vision that will bring about a significant transformation of our identity; we want it to happen now; *We want it all and we want it now*, as the song goes. Invariably, though, we run into obstacles along the way, challenges we could never imagine. So our progress is halted or diverted, and in many cases reversed. We get discouraged and start telling ourselves that we are undeserving or powerless or inept or we had an unrealistic vision. We lower our vision and our expectations to compensate. The negative voice in our internal dialogue takes over. 'I'm not being realistic,' we tell ourselves. But patience is what is called for. What is patience? It is the capacity for delayed gratification, and it opens up *humungous* possibilities when we learn how to get in touch with it. We might say that our vision is about our destination, but patience, along with living in the present, is about the journey, and the journey is everything."

Jerry sat, nodding in understanding. "I have to agree that patience is critically important. As I think back on the challenges in my life, it was a lack of patience that always caused me to give up. I somehow thought failure was justified. I just realized that I have been so results-oriented all my life, and while I know in some cases that's good, it has also caused me to compromise what I desired. I inevitably got something less than what I really wanted at the expense of waiting. Sometimes I felt that the end or result justified the means, which left me with a hollow achievement. I never thought about it that way until you described what patience means."

"And if we look again at the organizational gardening analogy and how plants grow, the vision, purpose, and passion might be compared to the sun, which gives direction and energy to the plant," Jennifer added. "The process would be the building and division of cells and the way water and nutrients move up the plant to nourish the cells. But somehow, patience has been built into a plant's nature. It's not even a question. You can't rush a tomato plant's growth. It happens when it happens. And here is another important point: things in nature usually start very small and initially grow very slowly. They start with a seed, and the rate of change is very gradual for a period of time. As I mentioned, the California sequoia takes eight years just to germinate! So there you have it. Patience may be most important at the start of our journey, but it's critical throughout the entire trip."

Thinking about his garden, Jerry said, "That is very true in my garden. The fruit of my effort won't happen for several weeks, even months. If I treated the plants like I treated a lot of my other endeavors, I would have dug the whole garden up and gone to the grocery store and bought tomatoes whose only similarity to home-grown is shape and color, but certainly not taste or texture."

"Absolutely," Jennifer said, laughing. "That is a great comparison. Something else to consider when we think about patience is its close connection with the present."

"How so?" Jerry asked.

"Think about the times you've been impatient. Wasn't your head usually somewhere else? Weren't you either thinking about something in the past like 'Oh, I wish it was like then' or 'If I only had this or that.' Or, what is even more common, we are late for something or other or we want to be some place other than where we are at the present moment. I've learned that if I focus on appreciating the moment, the now, my impatience disappears. I remember a couple of years ago when I ran the LA marathon.. I was doing all right until about mile twenty-three. Then I became so involved with the fact that I still had three miles to run I mentally gave up. From there on my pace was all messed up because my head, not my body, gave up. If I had just focused on the present, I would have done a lot better."

"Yeah, I can see what you're saying, but aren't you contradicting what you've said before about vision? Isn't vision about living in the future?" Jerry asked, sounding perplexed.

"Yes, vision is like a reference point, a point on the horizon we are moving toward, like we might look at if we were lost at sea, hungry and thirsty, focusing on an island in the distance. We think about it or reference it because it gives us direction and energy. But if our heads and our bodies only live there, we will accomplish nothing, and that eventually will lead to discouragement. As I mentioned before, vision is about a destination, but patience and the present are about the journey, and the journey is everything. We reach that distant island if we are patient, live in the moment, and, most important, continue to row toward it."

"I think I understand, but I need to toss all of this around in my head. There's a lot of information here. I need to put it all in perspective," Jerry said. "By the way, was the meal OK?"

"The meal was great. Let me help you clean up," Jennifer volunteered.

Chapter Sixteen

Our Core Opportunities

*A*fter the dishes were put away and they were seated in the living room, Jennifer said, "Jerry, it's getting late and I must go soon, but there's one last point I'd like to make before we call it a night. This will pretty much complete the major ideas behind Mary's self-cultivation philosophy. It's an important part of what we have been talking about, and it is something we can practice every day. It not only helps us move toward the identity we want to have, but it's also a key part of that identity.

"And what's that?" Jerry asked.

"It's about being honest with ourselves, and it's about observing ourselves," Jennifer replied. "Don't take me wrong, but do you believe you are always honest with yourself?"

"Well, of course," Jerry responded immediately.

"We'll see. Here's a paper and pen. Please write down five of your 'core opportunities,' personal characteristics you'd like to improve."

"My core what?" he asked.

"Your core opportunities. Here, I'll give you a couple of examples," Jennifer said. "I believe very strongly that listening empathically to others is very important, but I find myself too often behaving differently, thinking about something else while a person is talking, or thinking about what I'm going to say if the person would just shut up and let me have the stage. I don't like this behavior when I see it in others, so why should I act that way myself? But to change, I must be conscious of my behavior, and I must be honest with myself that I have a problem. I wish I were as good of a listener as you are. So at times there is a gap between what I say I believe and how I act or behave. If you recall Tom's barking dogs story, one of his core opportunities was eliminating his dislike of the barking sound."

Jennifer took the pen and drew two circles with a double-pointed arrow between them. In one circle she wrote I *believe* and in the other she wrote I *behave*. On the arrowed line she wrote *gap*. She then made five long lines underneath the diagram and handed the paper to Jerry.

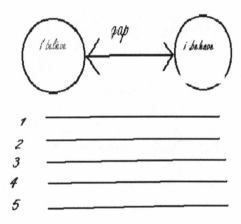

"Another example," she continued, "is that I believe that I should be patient and in control in all circumstances. But very often I find myself in a situation like sitting in traffic, you know, and I get restless and twitchy and my internal dialogue starts talking about the other drivers in negative ways, like what you mentioned the other night at Mary's. I sometimes act the same way standing in a long line at the grocery store. So, again, there is a gap between how I want to behave and how I too often actually act. You don't have to fill this in now; you don't have to fill it in at all. But to improve those behaviors we experience numerous times each day where a gap exists, it is important we first admit we have a problem and then become conscious of how we are acting so that we can catch ourselves and attempt to close the gap. These opportunities are behaviors we frequently experience, that is, on a daily basis. As we improve in each of them, we impact our ability to improve overall, and we increase our personal power. Again, we should go back to the pyramid of change and see ourselves acting the way we want to act."

Jerry took the pen and paper and said, "Let me see if I understand what you are saying. Aren't you talking about the second and fourth levels of the learning pyramid, behavior and belief? The problem is that even though we believe in a certain behavior and even see it as part of our desired identity, we may not have the ability to practice it at all times."

Jennifer responded, "That's true, but I think the real problem is that the desired behavior has not become habit. Since habit is defined as the combination of skills, knowledge, and desire, maybe we haven't had the sufficient desire and practice to make it a habit. Remember our discussion of the subconscious and the way it tends to act the way our conscious mind programs it to act? We've had a lot of bad programming over the years. There're many scars from the past, the negative feedback we give ourselves being the most common. Reprogramming our subconscious may take a while because of all the years we bombarded it with other beliefs. We may never completely close the gaps, but narrowing them is what is important. Again, the first thing we must do is admit we've a problem, that is, be honest with ourselves."

"You know, Jennifer," Jerry said thoughtfully, "this reminds me of the feedback forms management has us fill out on each other at work. Although they are anonymous, I am always skeptical that people don't necessarily put down the truth. And even if they do, unless I admit to myself that I have a problem and believe I should do something about it, all of that paper floating around is just a waste of time."

"You are absolutely right, Jerry," Jennifer said. "Wouldn't it make a lot more sense if we taught people to be honest about their behavior? I think that deep down most of us know what our major deficiencies are. The problem is doing something about them. This core-opportunity exercise is about just that."

"Well, I need to change my previous response," Jerry said. "No, I am not honest with myself, but I'm going to be. I have written *patience* and *negativity*. And I'm going to add *listening*. You may think I'm a good listener, but all of this stuff is so fascinating that it's easy to be enthralled. Sometimes at work I know I drift off, particularly when Andy is droning on about some great thing or other he has done. I'll have to think about what the others are."

"Well, it's getting late," Jennifer said, looking at the clock on the wall. "I need to get going. Thanks so much for dinner. I had a great time."

"I'm the one to be thanking you, Jennifer. I've fed you halibut, salad, and champagne, but you've given me a tremendous amount of food for thought. My tomato brain is soaking it up. Your insights are priceless."

"You're more than welcome," Jennifer responded, as she opened the door to leave. "I hope we can continue our discussion another time."

"I second that," Jerry said.

Chapter Seventeen

The New Role

*J*erry woke Sunday morning a little late. He had sat around awhile after Jennifer left, thinking about what she had said. It all made sense. In fact, this was no rocket science, to use a much overused expression; it was all pretty much common sense. But common sense is not always common practice. He was so excited about what they had discussed and the impact it could have that he hadn't gone to sleep until about 1:00, The clock showed 9:30, time to get up! He picked up a sheet of paper from the table beside the bed. On the page with his core opportunities he had written self cultivation in large letters at the top. He had written vision in large letters underneath. He had also written personal power and the Seven P's: purpose, passion, process, pace, progress, present, and, most important, patience. He had also drawn a pyramid with the five levels written in: environment, behavior, ability, beliefs, and values, and, at the top, identity. All of this, along with personal power, was evidently what Mary was referring to when she talked about self-cultivation.

After breakfast he found some bean poles in the garage to prop up the tomato plants and bean plants as Jennifer had advised. As he looked over his garden, he noticed some unwanted guests had started to grow among the vegetables. Weeds! As he pulled them up, he thought how they might represent the negative behavior we try to drive out to close the gap in our core opportunities. He recalled another opportunity for the list, procrastination. He must remember to add this to his list. He thought about how each time we impact one of our core opportunities we are adding to our personal power. All of these ideas were interconnected.

By the time he finished with his garden and some other chores around the house, it was late afternoon. He ate an early dinner of the leftover halibut. He opened a novel he had begun, and before he knew it, he had dozed off. Waking at about 10:00, he thought *I might as well turn in; I need to catch up on my sleep and be fresh at work tomorrow,* so he flipped off the light and slept soundly all night.

Jerry was not the only one who had had an introspective weekend. Blackburn had spent the time thinking about what Jerry had said and how these ideas might help change the culture at Microprojects. Before leaving on Friday, he had reviewed HR's work record on Jerry and found it to be impeccable. He also talked to Andy Mills and Jerry's previous boss. Both had nothing but favorable comments. If he had had an opening for another supervisor, Jerry would be a prime candidate. However, there were too many supervisors already. Besides, Joe saw another position was needed in the organization. His intuition was crying out that Jerry might be the right one for this role. But he needed to check something else. Jerry had said that he'd learned most of the ideas from the people at The Green Patch Nursery and that the owner had made him an apprentice. Maybe he'd stop by and see for himself. Of course, it was just a nursery, not a huge, complicated organization like Microprojects, but it might still be worth seeing.

Joe arrived at the nursery early Saturday morning. Two things grabbed him immediately. The first was the number of people; cars were everywhere. *Business must be good,* he thought. Second, there was a large colorful sign at the entrance that read:

The Green Patch Nursery

We Treat our Customers as

Well as our Plants

Come in and See!

Interesting! Joe thought. As he walked through the nursery, he noticed everything was laid out neatly and the place was spotless. The plants were so inviting that he wanted to take some home. Every time he passed one of the employees he got a big, warm, friendly smile, a sight he saw rarely at Microprojects. They seemed to be enjoying their work. He had stopped and was looking at several colorful hibiscus plants when he noticed beside him an orange "push" button with a sign under it that read:

Need Help? Push the button.
An associate will be right with you.

Joe decided to give it a try. He pushed the button and waited. Forty-five seconds later, a young man with *Tom* on his name tag walked up to Joe and asked, "Can I help you, sir?"

Joe, a little surprised and not necessarily ready to ask a question since he had only been testing the system, thought for a moment and said, "I'm admiring the hibiscus; they are beautiful. I was wondering if they are difficult to keep."

Tom responded "If you live in an area that gets frost, they need to be covered or protected, because if the temperature drops to freezing, it is apt to kill them. Once established they do better, but freezing weather requires that they are covered. The buds are very prone to aphids, so you need to apply insecticide or wash them off with a light spray of water. The blossoms are beautiful, but they don't last more than a day or two; however, they are profuse. On an established plant, the short flower life doesn't matter since the plant produces so many blossoms. The flower has a very unusual shape, don't you think? We have them in a variety of colors."

"Beautiful! Thank you," Joe said. "That was very helpful."

"You're welcome," Tom said. "Remember, we guarantee our plants for one year if you follow the instructions on the tag. Can I help you with anything else?"

"No, that should be all for now. I like your system for getting help," Joe commented.

"It's worked out very well. You will find these call buttons throughout the nursery," Tom replied. "If you need help, just ask any of our associates or push the button, and someone will be right with you."

Joe continued to peruse the tables of plants throughout the nursery. He was amazed at how fresh and vibrant everything looked.

All the plants were presented with such taste. As he wandered into an area where a multitude of orchids were displayed, he noticed a nursery employee with a long ponytail down to her waist. He recalled Jerry saying that the owner's name was Mary and that she usually worked on the floor with the other associates. *I wonder if that's her* he thought, so he walked up to her and said, "Excuse me, can you help me? I have a question about the orchids."

The lady started like he had surprised her, turned around and gazed at Joe for a few moments in a way that seemed as if she were reading his soul, and then she smiled and said in a most pleasant voice, "Sure. What do you need to know?"

Joe immediately noticed *Mary* on the left side of her shirt and the same tomato-like patch on the right side, the same picture he had seen on the sign outside the nursery. He said, "I'm interested in getting an orchid, but I know nothing about them. I thought I might start with something not too difficult. Are any of them easy to care for?"

Again she looked intently at him for a few moments as if she could see he had had no intention of buying an orchid or anything else, and then said, "Often 'ease' is a function of desire. But if you've never grown orchids you might consider one of the Cymbidiums," as she pointed to several pots of orchids with long, green, spear-like leaves and long stems with profuse flower growth. "They're relatively easy, have long-lasting blossoms as do most orchids, and give off a wonderfully subtle sweet fragrance."

"I think that's just what I'm looking for," Joe replied.

Mary smiled and said, "They like indirect or short periods of direct sun. Avoid placing them by a window that gets a lot of sun. Water them when the soil dries out a little, every week or so. The flowers should last for another month or two. The challenge is to get them to bloom again next season. They will need to be fertilized with orchid fertilizer, which we have on aisle seven. Follow the instructions on the tag or give us a call if you need help. Will there be something else?" she asked.

"No, you've been very helpful." He started to leave but turned to her and asked, "One thing, though. What's the significance of that tomato patch on your shirt? It is a tomato, isn't it?"

Mary replied, "Yes, it's a tomato and it's a part of our logo and a reminder of how we need to think and learn."

"I see," said Joe as Mary gave him another look as if she knew he didn't see at all. He said, "Well, thanks for your help." He picked up the potted cymbidium, stopped by aisle seven for the fertilizer, then walked to the front of the store to pay. He noticed there were no lines at check-out even though the store was very crowded. *What a well-run, customer-oriented place,* he thought as he drove home. His intuition was screaming louder than ever that Jerry was the right choice, particularly if Mary was his mentor. But his intuition was telling him something else, too; he felt that somehow Mary had known exactly who he was and why he was at the nursery.

Arriving early at work, Jerry found an unusual message on his answering machine. Blackburn wanted to meet with him at 1:00 if Jerry had time. Jerry had a lot of work to do on several projects, but he could make time for Blackburn. *Hey, this is the second meeting with him in two weeks,* he thought. *I wonder what he wants to talk about this time?*

Jerry worked feverishly all morning, trying to get caught up with phone calls, e-mails, and calculations he needed on his projects. He had to make time for the meeting with Blackburn, and if it was anything like the last meeting, it might take all afternoon. Since time was pressing, he decided to skip lunch. At 12:05, Gene Larsen stuck his head in Jerry's office and said, "Hey, Jer, it's about time to eat."

"I can't Gene. I've got a ton of work and a meeting this afternoon at 1:00 that could last the rest of the afternoon. We need to get the order in for the equipment for the McCabe project if we're going to complete it on time."

"You have *another* meeting with Mad Man Mills?" Gene said, grinning maliciously.

"No, actually, it's with Blackburn," Jerry responded a little too quickly, and then realized he had made a mistake sharing information like this with Gene. He would have a distorted version of it spread all over the site in an hour.

"Hoooo-weeee," Gene said as he shook his hand like he had just painted his fingernails. "Aren't we the important one."

"Cut it out, Gene," Jerry said, getting a little irritated. But he caught himself and thought, *Gene doesn't mean any harm. He's just having some fun.* "Oh, Blackburn probably just wants to know how you've been performing, see if you are ready to replace Mills. Don't worry; I won't tell him the truth; I'll make something up. You'll be a shoo-in for the job, although I will dislike working for you more than I do Mills," Jerry said with better humor.

"Great! I'll start packing the things in my office. I gotta look in to getting some gaudy modern art like Mills 'masterpieces,' " Gene panned. "Sure you don't have time for lunch?"

"No, Gene. I'll catch you later and fill you in," Jerry said as he went back to work.

Jerry arrived a few minutes early at Blackburn's office. He was feeling more confident, but he still had butterflies. Anita Evans said that Joe was waiting for him and he could go in. When Jerry opened the door, Joe got up from his desk and walked over and extended his hand.

"Thanks again for coming on short notice. I've been thinking about some things over the weekend that I'm anxious to share. Come in and sit down. Want some coffee or a soda?" Joe asked as he motioned Jerry over to the couch and chair in the corner of the room.

"No thank you, sir. I'm fine," Jerry responded, surprised that Blackburn would want to share his thoughts with him. Jerry detected a subtle sweet fragrance in the air and noticed a large potted orchid in the corner of the room he hadn't seen on his previous meeting with Joe.

After both were seated, Joe looked seriously at Jerry and said, "Jerry, I've been giving a lot of thought to what you said last week about turning the pyramid upside-down and all that stuff about organizational gardening and self-cultivation. I think you re onto something, Jerry. So I've an offer for you."

All Jerry could say was, "Yes sir?"

"I think we need to start a cultivation program here at Microprojects," he continued. "As I mentioned before, I've been trying to work through my staff here to bring about an empowered work force, but to be honest, I don't think they know 'diddly about turning an organization upside-down; heck, most of them got where they are by being good at command and control. The whole empowerment thing seems to be more of a threat to them than a new, better way of being organized. I've been searching and reading and thinking about what to do for some time now. I'm very impressed by the 'learning organization' concepts put forth in Peter Senge's book, *The Fifth Discipline,* which I just finished reading. And then in you pop, and I think, 'This guy has his head in the right place; this just might be the answer I've been seeking.'

"Your work record here as a project manager has been excellent, and I like the way you handled yourself at the meeting on the Felton Project. You come across as being knowledgeable and confident but not arrogant. Those are rare traits. So here's my offer, and I do want to emphasize that it is an offer. The decision of whether to do it is entirely up to you. It's not a command. I'd like you to put together a proposal for how we'd start transforming the organization using ideas like we discussed last week and, with my full support, lead the effort. I want the staff to hear it first. It's imperative that we include them from the start. The change of mind-set must begin with them. As I said, you will have my support, one hundred percent, and I mean that. Jim Crabtree, our CEO, is coming here in six weeks. I want to lay out our plans for the organization changes for him, which means we don't have a lot of time. So what do you think?"

Jerry's immediate reaction was *I can't do it. It's too big for me! I don't know enough!* He said, "But . . ." Then he thought about his habit of negativity and continued, ". . . how would we be able to handle all the projects I've got going?"

"The projects are important," Joe responded. "But changing culture in this organization is more important. I'll ask Mills to assign them to someone else. We've lots of engineers who could take them on; don't worry about that. I'd like a draft proposal from you in four weeks about how you would go about changing the mind-set, about how this 'gardening' would take place."

"Yes, sir" Jerry said. "But I need to understand upfront what my boundaries are, what I'll be responsible for."

"Your responsibility will be to lead the effort and train my staff in the concepts of what you call 'organizational gardening'. I expect you to review the program with me before you start. After we have run a pilot program with the staff, I expect you to train the rest of the organization. You may recruit whomever you need to help you, but pass it by me before you commit to anyone. As a first start, let's say your budget will be two hundred thousand dollars. How's that sound?"

"I'll give it my best, sir," Jerry said, feeling a little overwhelmed. Good thing Jennifer had helped him out over the weekend. But he would still need to get a lot of coaching and advice from Mary about the other facets of organizational gardening and what the best approach should be.

"Great, Jerry," Joe said, extending his hand. "By the way, I'm raising your pay and promoting you to a level commensurate with the rest of the staff. I'll announce it to them in the morning and then make the announcement to the whole site, so please don't say anything to anyone until then. Your title will be Organizational

Development Leader. I thought about the title of Head Gardener, but I doubt they are ready for that just now. If you need anything, please call. Can I have a status report in two weeks? Is that too soon?"

"If I know anything about organizational gardening, *you* are the head gardener, sir. Anyway, it's a lot to do in a short period of time, but as long as it's a status report, no problem," Jerry said, sounding more positive than he was feeling. "Thanks very much! This is very exciting. Thanks for having the confidence in me to trust me with this kind of responsibility!"

"Jerry, some may consider this a rash decision on my part. It's natural for people to question what may appear to be an off-the-cuff decision. But I've looked at your record and discussed your performance with Andy and others. Surprisingly enough, the most successful decisions I've made have been based on gut feel. Not that they were made in a vacuum—I've listened and observed and studied. I don't mean to sound arrogant, but few of these decisions have failed. I have complete confidence this one won't either. I'll support you the whole way and help facilitate your getting the right resources if you need my help. I'm just thankful this opportunity exposed itself like it did."

"So you might say that intuition is part of your personal power," Jerry laughed.

"My personal what?" Joe asked, quizzically.

"Your personal power, sir; it's the nutrient of self-cultivation," Jerry responded.

"Well, I'll look forward to learning about it," Joe said, smiling, "that and a lot of other things. See you later," he said as he walked Jerry to the door with his hand on his shoulder.

Jerry walked back to his office in a daze; first the dinner with Mary and her friends and all he learned there, then Jennifer and her valuable insights, and now this—what a turn of events. *A position commensurate with the other staff,* Joe had said. Mills was not his boss anymore! *But how could I possibly change the culture of Microprojects?* he asked himself. The task seemed daunting as doubts flooded his mind. As he sat in his office pondering the magnanimity of it all, he recalled what he had learned from Mary the first couple of times he had talked to her: *The two important needs are the "want to" and the "how to" within the boundary of our authority.* Well, he now would have the authority, and the desire, the "want to," was increasing with each moment. What he needed to do was learn more from Mary about the organizational gardening she did at the nursery and duplicate it at Microprojects. *Let's see,* he thought, *the purpose, passion, process, progress, pace, the present, and patience.* Well, he certainly had a purpose, and the passion was building; he would need to enlarge on and understand the processes by talking to Mary, Natalie, and Jennifer. But patience? What did Jennifer say? *Passion can sometimes be the enemy of patience,* or was it the opposite? He would need to be careful and not get too anxious, take his time and not move too fast. He needed to start by building strong roots by studying and learning as much as he could about the process, much as some plants establish a strong root system before anything visible appears above ground.

Jerry grabbed his list of phone numbers and called Mary. He told her about his meeting with Blackburn and his new role. She congratulated him and said, "So, Blackburn's not as bad as you thought?" He agreed that Joe wasn't anything like what he'd imagined. Jerry asked her if he could see her and find out more about the particulars of organizational gardening beyond what she had already told him. He said he understood the self-cultivation part pretty well, although he wasn't all that proficient at practicing it. But he felt he needed to find out a lot more about how an organization can create an environment that allows its employees to thrive. She agreed there was more she could share with him. He mentioned the relatively narrow timeline he must work in, and she agreed to meet with him at her house the following weekend in the evening. She would ask Natalie and Jennifer to be there too to provide their perspectives. She asked him to read several articles on related subjects in the meantime. As he thought about the prospect of seeing Jennifer and Natalie again and learning more about what he needed to be effective in his new role, he took on a pleasant anticipation of the weekend meeting. *Too bad it's only Monday. Four more days to wait.* Then he reminded himself: *patience.*

Chapter Eighteen

The "Supposed to be" and the "Awe"

*J*erry was sitting in his office early the next morning, trying to figure out how he was going to pass along his projects to someone else without letting something slip through the cracks when Gene Larson walked in and sat down. "How's it going, Jer? So, what was the big meeting with Blackburn about? I stopped by several times yesterday but you weren't around. It must've been real important stuff to be in there all afternoon. Your tail doesn't look like it's been singed, so it must be some juicy stuff."

"No, it wasn't about that at all, but it was an interesting meeting, Gene. But I'm sorry I can't say what it's about right now. Though I can say that I'll let you know later today," Jerry replied.

"Ah, come on, Jer. Can't you give me a hint?" Gene whined. "No one spends the afternoon in Blackburn's office unless it's something big. I'm dying to find out. Is it about Mills? Was Blackburn trying to find out whether Mills is a complete jerk like everyone knows? I hope you told him the truth. I'd love to see the door hitting him in the tail!"

"No, it wasn't about that and, besides, I think Blackburn realizes that Andy has a lot of good qualities. You'll just have to wait, Gene. You'll just have to be patient," Jerry said, smiling.

Gene left Jerry's office shaking his head and looking disappointed. He walked across the hall and started talking to some of the other engineers, looking over at Jerry's office every so often. Gene had the reputation of being the main grape on the office grapevine, and if he couldn't get the real scoop, he would probably just make something up. Jerry wondered what kind of wild story Gene was concocting, then he realized he better get back to work.

Late in the morning, the announcement was put out via e-mail and broadcast over the site's closed-circuit TV by Blackburn himself. He said that Jerry Artson was assuming a new role of Organizational Development Leader. He went on to say that the Santa Clara Microprojects site was to be a pilot for the company's move to a more empowered organization and that Jerry would be leading the effort. Blackburn said that every employee would be involved and that they would be hearing more in the weeks to come. Several of the engineers, including Gene, stopped by and congratulated Jerry. Even Mills called to offer his congratulations, saying that Jerry should not worry about the projects he was working on; Mills would transfer those to other engineers. He said that Blackburn had directed him to "free Jerry up ASAP."

The rest of the week was very busy. Jerry worked with three of the other project engineers and Andy to transfer his projects to them. All of them showed Jerry a degree of reverence that he was not used to and, for sure, not comfortable with.

In the evening Jerry read some of the articles Mary had recommended. On Saturday, he stopped by his office to finish straightening up his files and went to Mary's in the afternoon. He had been too busy during the week to think much about the meeting with her, but as he drove to her house he was looking forward to seeing her again. The more he thought about the awesome responsibility he had been given, the more he worried. Initially he had been excited, but now he felt maybe he had been too quick accepting Blackburn's offer. Maybe some time with Mary would help him sort things out.

Mary had told him that she would probably be working in the yard and to come on back if no one answered the door. Jerry found her outside behind the house on her knees, working in a large flowerbed. The colors were beautiful in the afternoon sun. He had begun to feel sullen and agitated, but the sight of Mary, the rich black soil, the flowers, and the golden glow of the sun took some of the edge off his negative demeanor. Mary turned when she heard Jerry approaching and said, "Hey, Jerry! It's nice to see you! How're things?"

Jerry frowned and responded, "Hi, Mary. What a crazy week this has been. I can hardly believe what has happened. As I said on the phone, I've been given the job of leading the company's move to empowerment. It was announced earlier in the week. I'm both exhilarated and apprehensive, and I've been going back and forth between the two. But I keep getting caught in the old self-doubt. One day I'm Mr. Project Engineer, just one of the masses, responsible for some things but nothing I can't handle. Now all of a sudden I'm expected to transform all of Microprojects; that's what culture change is, isn't it, Mary?" Jerry said in a panicky tone. "I'm smart enough to know that culture is almost impossible to change. And then those in power are so fixated on self importance. They're not going to give that up, Mary! None of this is going to work, not with those kinds of odds! I'm going to end up failing!" he whined.

Mary simply said, "It's normal what you're feeling about the fear of what you may encounter as you try to change the culture at Microprojects. Congratulations on the promotion. What an opportunity! What you're feeling is normal. I believe we can help you with the feeling of apprehension. The exhilaration should be welcomed, but be careful you don't wallow in it either, though; take it all in stride. You mind helping me plant some of these flowers?" she asked, abruptly changing the subject. "Natalie and Jennifer won't be here for a couple of hours; they're finishing some things up at the nursery."

Jerry, a little disappointed that the others would be late and that Mary seemed more interested in digging in the soil than sympathizing with his state, said, "No problem. Just show me what to do."

Mary replied, "This is pretty mundane work, Jerry. The 'how to' will be obvious. Sometimes there's nothing like mundane activity to relax your mind. And with all that you've been through lately, it'll be welcome. I remember that John used to say that mundane but strenuous work is one of the most relaxing things a person can do. See that retaining wall over there by the hill?" as she pointed at a wall about three to four feet high and a couple-hundred feet long composed of railroad ties. "John built that entirely by himself. He'd come home from school in the evening and start digging with a posthole digger, way into the evening, until it was so dark that he could barely see what he was doing. I asked him why he didn't get someone to help him and use a gas powered auger. It would have gone so much faster. He said digging the holes let him relax and think. He had been working for weeks on his research project . When John was focused on something he became non-communicative, totally into whatever he was doing. One evening when he was about finished with the wall he ran in shouting that he, 'had it'. He had figured out whatever it was that he couldn't get. He said it was earthshaking. What he had discovered would make a tremendous impact on the world of physics. John was rumored to receive an award for his discovery, but not long after that the plane crash happened" she said as her voice trailed off. Then she continued, "The mundane work he was doing digging somehow allowed him to make the discovery. So, who knows what you may come up with as you plant these flowers", she said smiling.

For the next hour they worked side by side. He felt his anxiety fade and a relaxed feeling come over him. Even though they worked in silence, Mary emanated charisma. There was a peacefulness about her that was contagious. Jerry had been thinking about Mary and the life she had led, and he had wanted to ask her something for a long time. Mary seemed to epitomize self-confidence, love of life, purpose, patience, and wisdom. If she could overcome the misfortunes that had befallen her, and end up in a state that would be the envy of anyone, then maybe he could deal with the obstacles that had been dropped in his own. Although she had just mentioned John, he wasn't sure if it was appropriate to ask her about him and her past, and he didn't know how to best broach the subject. Finally he said, "Mary, I've wanted to ask you something for a long time, but I'm not sure it's a subject you want to talk about. If you don't please say so, OK?"

What is it, Jerry?" she asked, smiling.

"Well, uh . . ." he stammered, "You, uh, you never talk about your husband or your son. I've always been amazed how you had the strength to go on, seemingly unfazed by what happened. How, how, uh, have you managed to cope?"

There was a long silence during which Mary gazed off in the distance. Jerry worried that he had touched a forbidden subject.

He wasn't sure whether she was angry or sad, and he was about to apologize and tell her to never mind when she turned to him with a smile and said, "No, you are right I never talk about it, but that doesn't mean I mind. I don't mind in the least. I guess I don't bring it up because I don't want people to feel sorry for me or I don't want to burden people with my past. Sometimes they can act so strange when confronted with the subject of death. But now that you've asked, let me share this with you.

"I always thought I was very strong, but after John's plane crashed, I was thrown into a state of depression that made me, at times, suicidal. I can think of no greater loss than the loss of a spouse or a child. But when both happen, nothing compares with that. Nothing, Jerry!" she said as her expression took on a momentary look of sadness.

She regained her composure and continued, "The loss of a parent or a friend is difficult enough, but the sorrow and loss and emptiness and confusion and guilt, yes, guilt, I felt was much deeper than when either of my parents passed away. Death is so final; that's the hard part, coming to terms with the reality that I would never see them again. I'd go back over my behavior and wish I'd acted different, but I couldn't go back. If I could have only a few moments, a few beautiful moments, with them again to say I was sorry for the way I had been, to express my deep unwavering love for both of them, but I couldn't. I couldn't. I felt like I was suffocating and claustrophobic, like one of those strange dreams when you know you are sleeping and something very scary is happening and you want to wake up but you can't. That is the closest I can come to describing it, but I was *awake*. I came up with a million reasons why I should have done something to alter what happened, that somehow it was my fault that the plane crashed. We were supposed to drive up the coast to Bodega Bay that weekend, but I had a paper to complete for school, so I cancelled the trip. John and Benny went flying, probably to get away from my foul mood. But I had cancelled our trip. I had run them off. I caused that plane to crash by selfishly thinking of myself rather than thinking of John and Benny.

"It must have been awful", Jerry interjected.

"It was. For a while I became a recluse; I had no desire to see or talk to anyone, and I started dwelling on the past as if it were the future. I felt I was losing my mind. If I could only go back and change all of the things I'd done to John and Benny, the times I'd been angry and moody and selfish and too demanding, and when I didn't listen, and on and on. Believe it or not, that is what I focused on rather than all the wonderful times we'd had together. I'd mope around and my feelings would alternate from anger at John for doing this—*He killed my son and left me here alone!*—to self blame, then on to self pity and supreme sorrow, and then around again and again."

Mary stopped and gazed off in the distance, thinking how to best continue. She looked over at Jerry, smiled, and went on. "I finally reached a point where I'd cried so much I didn't think I had any more tears. Then one day, when I thought I was at my rope's end, I recalled something John had said to me years before. It just sort of popped into my head from nowhere. It was right after we were married. I was in turmoil over a paper I was doing for a class I was taking. But it wasn't just that; I'd been complaining about a lot of things. One evening I was very depressed, and John sat down beside me. You recall, Jerry, that John was a physicist. Much of the time he seemed to live in a different dimension," she said, laughing. "Believe me, it can be a real challenge living with someone who spends a lot of time in the abstract. Part of the time I didn't know what he was talking about, and other times he didn't say anything. But don't get me wrong, Jerry. He was very loving and considerate most of the time. His curiosity only embellished his traits, but it was the way *I was feeling* at the time. Patiently, he asked me to consider something that always helped him when he was feeling down or when he was in the midst of an unfortunate event".

"What was that?, Jerry asked.

Mary replied, "He said that regardless of the situation, no matter how bad or how wonderful it is, the question we must ask ourselves is what have we learned. He cited as an example something I had almost forgotten. One afternoon before John and I were married, I was driving from San Francisco to Santa Cruz. The traffic was absolutely horrendous. It was stop-and-go the whole way. For a short stretch I was driving along at an almost normal speed when suddenly the traffic slowed again. All of a sudden my car jolted forward, and glass from the rear window sprayed all over the car. A large pickup going about fifty had rear-ended me. I staggered out of the car, which had been knocked over the left two lanes to the neutral ground, thinking it might catch fire. I felt dazed and disoriented. Several motorists stopped and helped me, and an ambulance came and took me to the San Jose hospital. After going through several tests, it was determined that I, miraculously, had come out of the incident unscathed; the car, however, was totaled. It took me several weeks to calm down from this near-death incident. I was so angry I wanted to sue the driver of the truck. Who'd he think he was, driving along in his big two-ton weapon; not paying attention? He'd almost killed me.

"I'm amazed you weren't hurt", Jerry stated.

"Me too! A few weeks later, John and I were discussing the incident. I was still on my 'get back at that idiot' stance, when John said to me that I had had a 'freebie'. I asked him what on earth he was talking about. I had almost been killed by some guy, driving a car twice the size of mine, because he was, obviously, not paying attention to driving, and John was calling it a 'freebie'. He patiently said that it was OK to feel anger or sadness or remorse about a situation like this, but at some point we have to move on and ask ourselves what we've learned. He said that he had asked himself the same question, and what he'd learned was that when we drive carelessly, we might inflict the type of injury that had happened to me on someone else. He said he realized that too often he tailgated cars when he was in a hurry, and the potential impact of this had never hit home as hard as when he saw what'd happened to me. He said that he too had had a freebie, that is, an important lesson that was easier to understand because of the emotional impact it involved. He said that if I wanted to sue the guy I could, although I might have a hard time finding a lawyer to take the case, but before I did, I should examine my own driving habits and determine if there except for luck went I. It took a while for me to come to terms with what he was telling me, but eventually I had to admit that on many occasions I could've inflicted the same misfortune on someone else. It made a great impact on the way I drive, and to this day I always drive a safe distance behind the car in front of me.

"But although I drove more safely because of what had happened, I had forgotten about learning from every occasion, and

I had forgotten something else John had once said, which was that 'Most people go through life believing that every occasion is either a blessing or curse, but people in control of their lives see every occasion as an opportunity to learn.' As I pondered my miserable existence after John and Benny's deaths, I thought back on all of this. I gradually came to realize I had spent enough time mourning and wallowing in self pity. Was it possible that I could turn it into a learning experience? At first it seemed so demeaning of John and Benny. It took awhile to see my personal tragedy as a lesson, but eventually I did".

"What was the lesson", Jerry asked.

"I learned that as I looked back on my behavior after Jon and Benny's deaths, I realized I was spending considerable time wishing I had acted differently while they were here. The powerful lesson was that you should live your life such that, regardless of what happens, you have nothing to regret or be sorry for. Just like years before, when I had learned from the traffic incident that I should use it as a motivation to drive more carefully, I realized I should conduct my life in a way that I'd minimize my regrets and sorrows. But that was the opposite of what I was doing by spending my time as a recluse, wallowing in self pity, turning off the few friends who John and I had by refusing to see them, friends who if anything happened to them, I would again be sorry and remorseful that I hadn't acted differently.

"But the more I thought about it, the more I realized that this was not the only lesson I could draw from this unfortunate event. As I thought back on my behavior, I realized I had been living totally in the past. What if I tried to live in the moment? This is when I discovered the 'awe' and the 'supposed-to-be'. The more I examined my life, the more I became convinced that I had been living in some kind of soap opera, something I had seen on TV or in a movie. People were *supposed* to act this way. This is the way things were *supposed* to be. I call this the supposed to be; all of those ideas about the world that have been drilled into our heads since birth, many of which are flawed, like the idea the Europeans had about the tomato when it was first introduced to Europe. But the more I lived in the moment, the more I learned to observe, the more fascinated I became with the world around me in many, many ways.

I call this the *awe*. One reason this idea exposed itself, I suppose, is because John and Benny's death help me realize how valuable time is, how we should live each moment like it is our last. When I looked at it like this, the need to live in the supposed-to-be seemed such a waste of time, and the awe became so intriguing.

"Now I look back over my life with John as a beautiful learning experience. I wouldn't have thought it possible, but even the death of him and Benny was a powerful lesson. Perhaps most of all, I stopped wallowing in self pity. And that was the way I started to live. I was gradually able to come out of my reverie of self-pity, anger, and blame. I realized that we have only two choices: change the situation or change the way we look at it; no other choice exists. And the choice was mine, so that was when I decided to do both, that was when I decided to buy the nursery. Why a nursery? Because I've always loved growing things and because nature is the most awesome thing there is, and, to me, nature is best represented by a garden, by plants, by beautiful flowers. I also realized something I think I already knew: the same patterns that govern the plant world are present throughout nature. They are present in human beings. By looking at nature through the plant world, I was able to better understand myself.

"Like the insight I gained in how to deal with my boss by caring for my plants", asked Jerry.

"Right, Jerry. The freedom I have attained is infinite. You see, all we have is something we call *time*. We don't have any idea what it is, but we do know it is finite, and everything else is infinite. The awe is infinite, the freedom is infinite, the sorrow, anger, sadness, the choices, all are infinite. You can have all of them you want. If you start out right now and spend the rest of your days trying to understand the universe, you will only comprehend a small amount. But it will be worth it, Jerry, because I believe that learning is our calling. So time's a-wasting, Jerry, time's a-wasting."

Mary stopped and smiled at Jerry. His challenge at Microprojects seemed infinitesimally petty compared to what Mary had been through. He didn't know what to say, so he just said, "Thanks for sharing that with me. You are right, you know, Mary. But I hope I am never faced with what you have been through."

Mary replied, "I hope so too, Jerry. I hope so too. You know, our journey toward our vision might be represented by a person walking down a long hall." Mary drew a picture of a long hall in the dirt with a stick. "At the end of the hall is his vision, portrayed in cinemascope colors, very vivid and compelling. The person is inspired by the vision and is full of energy and desire. But as he walks toward his vision, something happens; he encounters a large obstacle in his path that halts his progress. As he looks around he notices a door on the wall of the hall beside him, and behind him he sees that the entrance to the hall is locked and he can't return. To reach his vision he must somehow pass the obstacle, or he can exit through the side door. But outside the hall there is no vision, and to exit may mean he must start all over, either that or give up and quit altogether. He is filled with a passion for his vision, so he decides to squeeze through a narrow opening at one corner of the obstacle only to find after a few paces another obstacle with another exit door in his path. Throughout his journey he encounters numerous obstacles, each with an exit door. Some of the obstacles he can squeeze around or scale, but others are like an enormous wall that he must chip apart, bit by bit. But something happens along the way; he discovers that the removal of the obstacle is almost as compelling as the vision itself. He is filled not only with a passion for reaching his vision but a passion for embracing every obstacle, every challenge.'

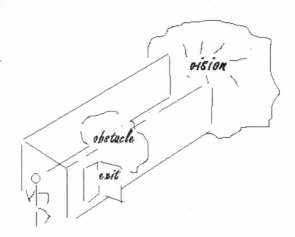

"It's not particularly easy to reach such a mind-set, Jerry, but the rewards are tremendous. Unfortunately, many people choose the door. Why? Because it's there, because it's easy, because . . . Who knows? But after exiting, they turn around and see written on the outside the words, 'No entrance for failures.' They believe it means them, so they choose to not reenter. But the words are only words, and the choice to reenter or not is just that, a choice. They confirm they are failures simply because they choose to believe they are failures, to follow the 'supposed-to-be'. What's really peculiar, Jerry, is that many of the obstacles people encounter are only in their head; they create them. They create them, perhaps, like the obstacle you are creating; the one about you failing in your new job. Since you are free to create in your mind, why not create a vision of yourself succeeding instead?"

Mary smiled at Jerry, and her piercing green eyes momentarily grabbed hold of him, and he felt a strange feeling in his midsection. He realized how totally absurd he had been acting, but more than that he was filled with a renewed sense of the power he had to master his own fate, to turn this new obstacle into an experience, a learning experience, a challenge, another opportunity for growth. It was like an enormous burden had been lifted off his shoulders. He felt a need to release his emotions. He looked over at Mary and smiled and she smiled back at him with such understanding that his smile turned into a laugh, then Mary started giggling, and they both began to laugh. Jerry started laughing so hard he was afraid he was going to convulse. At one point he couldn't get his breath, and every time he looked at Mary it only got worse. He got up and walked over behind a tree. Able at last catch his breath, he was still howling when Jennifer and Natalie arrived and Jennifer said, "It must have been a real knee-slapper. Would anyone let us in on the joke?"

"It was about nothing," Jerry gasped, and then he and Mary both cracked up laughing again.

Jennifer and Natalie joined in and laughed almost as hard as Mary and Jerry, which only goes to show you that it's easy to laugh about nothing.

Chapter Nineteen

Learning the "How-To" of Organizational Gardening

When everybody had calmed down, Mary volunteered to fix some snacks. They would meet in the library. Jerry walked there with Jennifer while Natalie and Mary prepared the food. The library was larger than Jerry remembered. Shelves containing hundreds and hundreds of books and stacks of periodicals lined one of the walls. Several large modern paintings adorned another. At the center of the third wall was a large granite fireplace, with more bookshelves on each side. The fourth wall framed a large picture window that looked out on the beautiful landscaped grounds and the fading evening light. Two comfortable sofas and several cushioned armchairs in earth-tone colors surrounded a large, low, modern glass coffee table that was somehow balanced on four granite rocks. Stacked on the table were several books and magazines.

"This is my favorite room," Jennifer said. "It gets a lot of use. I love to come here when it's rainy or cold outside and just sit and read. With a nice fire in the fireplace you couldn't find a more pleasing ambiance anywhere, so comfortable and inviting."

Jerry collapsed on one of the sofas. "Yes, I'd forgotten how nice it is here. You think Mary has read all these books?" he asked, scanning the shelves.

"I think she probably has read a lot of them, but she always says modestly that she can't remember any of them," Jennifer responded. "There's quite a collection: art, history, numerous novels both recent and classical, plus a lot of John's science books and Mary's multitude of gardening and plant books."

"We were discussing John earlier this afternoon. She mentioned something he had taught her years ago about using every occasion as an opportunity to learn," Jerry said.

"I'd say that Mary epitomizes someone who is fascinated with the world. She never appears to be bored, always reading or working on something. She has somehow reached a state where she is totally attentive to whatever she's doing. Have you noticed that when she is working on something and you walk up to her that you often surprise her?"

"Yes," Jerry replied, "now that you mention it."

"Well, I think it's caused by her attentiveness, her absorption in what is at hand, her focus, her awe with everything. Having lived with her for several months, I've come to realize that she is that way about everything she does, whether she's cooking or reading or eating or planting flowers or in conversation with someone. Have you noticed that when you talk to her she never interrupts? She seems to hang on to every word you are saying, like what you have to tell her is tremendously important. I think it is all part of her sense of fascination with the world. And she is always so calm and so much in control. It is a state of behavior that I admire. She told me something once. It was after she had introduced the idea of observation. I was having trouble applying the concept; I was finding it difficult to stop my internal dialogue. She said that since she had been spending more time observing, she had been able to 'see' more often. She said it was uncanny how often her 'seeing' was supported by her observations. She told me that even though it was still being interpretive, it was at a much higher level. It was a sense of what was taking place, a place where there was an absence of labels. She said it happens when we learn to turn off our internal dialogue. She called it 'stopping the world'. "

"Very interesting," said Jerry "She mentioned something about stopping the world one time when I came upon her gazing at the roses at the nursery. She said in an environment like that, it is easy to do. Have you ever been able to stop the world?"

"More and more I try to force myself to observe, to focus, and shut up in my mind. When I do, it is very relaxing, and I learn a lot more. I'm getting better, but I'm a long way from the state Mary achieves. I can't say that I've ever stopped the world, though."

"Me neither," said Jerry. He turned his head as Natalie and Mary entered the room. The two were carrying trays of food and a bottle of wine.

"Nothing special," Mary said. "Something to nibble on if anyone gets hungry."

"OK," Jennifer and Jerry said in unison as they reached for sandwiches on the tray.

"Now," Mary said, sitting down in one of the armchairs, propping her feet on the coffee table, and pouring herself a glass of wine. "Let's see if we can give Jerry what he needs to put together a learning program for his new job. Jerry, over the last few weeks, you have learned about self-cultivation. It is always of primary importance because it starts preparing you to be able to deal with just about any situation. For this reason, it is the first thing that should be learned. Self-cultivation is about creating your own environment; it's about the thinking tomato. The other part, which we call organizational gardening, is what we will discuss tonight. It is about creating the optimum environment for tomatoes to think. Please feel free to take notes if you like. Natalie, would you like to start?"

"Sure," Natalie responded. "Either of you chime in anytime you like. And, Jerry, please question anything you don't understand."

"Organizational gardening," she began, "as we have mentioned before, is about making it easier for everyone to have the 'want to' and the 'how to' in order to grow and develop to meet the organization's needs and their own needs. It is analogous to providing the right soil, water, sunlight, and temperature conditions for a plant to grow. It doesn't guarantee growth, but it does greatly increase the probability that growth will occur. When we talk about the future, and this is very important, there are no guarantees; we can only increase or decrease the probability that something will happen.

"The first area is called learning. It may be the most important nutrient in the organization's soil, because all development and growth comes from learning. It is about acquiring knowledge and skills. In the end, knowledge always wins, always has and always will. Brute strength and force may make a temporary impact, but they will never stand up to knowledge. There are two parts to the learning environment. One encompasses the formal learning programs, such as classes or seminars; the other concerns the way people interact with each other, day in and day out.

"Let's look at the former," Natalie continued. "All learning programs should be done in a way that fits the learning skills of the participants. Some people prefer visual learning, some auditory, some spatial, and some may be hands-on learners, and so on. We use all of these, normally, but we may have a preference. The learning program should take this into account and not just use a one-size-fits-all approach that many companies and learning institutions fall back on."

"I'm not sure I understand what you mean," Jerry asked. "Can you give me an example?"

"The best example is the education system all of us experienced in grade school, high school, and college," Jennifer interjected. "Wasn't the learning system in most cases mainly lecture? That is, auditory with maybe a little visual, and a lot of reading with some hands-on lab work thrown in occasionally?"

"Yeah, most of it was, now that I think about it," said Jerry. "And most of it was pretty boring. I have always thought that of all the classes I took in high school and college, only a few were exciting. And, as I think about it, those were very participatory, hands-on, and we were allowed to practice what we learned."

"Exactly," said Jennifer. "Learning programs that maximize the transfer of knowledge include a variety of learning media: practice, games, music, three dimensions, and lots of participation and practice in a non-threatening environment."

"Music?" exclaimed Jerry, suddenly taking note of the classical music playing in the background.

"Yes, music," Mary confirmed. "It's all part of something called 'accelerated learning'. With the job you have ahead of you, I think it would behoove you to take a class. It would be very worthwhile. I have a friend who teaches the process, and she routinely gives weeklong seminars on the subject. Of course you will learn about it by participating in the accelerated learning process itself. From there, you may want to take some more classes and maybe read about it. I'll give you her name and you can call her."

"It sounds very interesting" Jerry said. "That was what one of the articles you gave me to read for tonight was about, wasn't it?"

"Yes," Mary said.

"I attended her seminar, and it was probably the best learning experience about learning I have ever had," said Natalie. "This is something we incorporate in all of our formal learning programs at The Green Patch. We conduct a lot of classes; most of it is about the particulars associated with growing various plants. To make it most effective, we use the accelerated learning process. We have all practiced it a lot, but it would be better if you learned firsthand through one of the experts. Now let's talk about the second part of the learning environment, the way people interact with each other. It is about making every interaction, every occasion, every meeting, and every discussion a learning experience."

"How can an organization influence that?" asked Jerry.

"By creating an environment in which people are encouraged to be both open and honest," said Jennifer. "Being honest is about saying what you're thinking rather than what you're expected to say or that you believe is politically correct. That doesn't mean that you're rude or disrespectful. You have to use some tact, but it does mean being honest about your opinions or perspective or ideas. Being honest doesn't necessarily mean you should just spout anything that comes to mind. It also means you should be careful about generalizations and interpretations that lack sufficient observation."

"I think I know what you mean," exclaimed Jerry. "It is amazing how much game playing goes on at work; people saying one thing at the water fountain or at lunch or after work when management isn't around, and then saying the exact opposite when talking to management in meetings or one-on-ones. And a lot of the time the same thing goes on between coworkers and, I am sure, between management. It's such a waste of time; it's like we are all living in a make-believe world. No one has any idea what the truth is. It is exasperating and such a waste of time!"

"That's true of a lot of communication," said Natalie. " The other half is the 'openness,'. "Not only do we have to say what is on our mind, but we have to be open to what the other person is saying, to listen empathetically without evaluating, to consider others' viewpoints as possible and viable. At the same time we should question generalizations and interpretations we don't understand."

"And if you think it is hard to be honest and say what you are really thinking in a way that is not offensive," Mary said, "well, it is one heck of a lot harder to be open. We are so tied to our view of the world, our mental models, our paradigms, that it is very difficult to admit that they might not be accurate. Our huge egos can be so fragile, sometimes, that even the suggestion that our view might not be accurate is enough to shatter it to pieces. Talk about being tied to the 'supposed-to-be'; our mental blindness destroys the 'awe'. Just saying that people in an organization should be candid and open is one thing, but to practice it in a meaningful way is a tremendous challenge. The single greatest impact is when an organization's leadership comes out and starts listening empathetically, when they set the example by admitting error, when they walk the talk and demonstrate that honesty and openness are the center of the organization's legitimacy not by what they preach but by their actions. This starts the proverbial snowball rolling, but not very fast because the trust level may be very low. People may have spoken out in the past only to find that they have been labeled troublemakers; they may have listened empathetically only to be used by someone's hidden agenda. It moves slowly at first, but gradually things begin to change."

"But how do you start the change?" asked Jerry.

"Like Mary said," Natalie responded. "You have to get the top leaders of the organization to change their behavior. They can't stay hidden in their offices. They must get out and interact with people. When open and honest dialogue takes place, the trust level will start to improve. This is where their patience will be tested. The habit of open and honest communication must become part of each leader's core-opportunity focus. Things that had been known but never talked about before will begin to sprout up all over. Of course, problems that have never been visible before will also begin to sprout. Actually, they were always there but they couldn't be seen, like . . . well, like the tomato worms on a tomato plant; they're ugly and damaging but they're hard to see, just like a lot of the problems in an organization. They are there, but management can't see them or won't admit they exist, or knows they are there but wants to hide them. Meanwhile, however, the damage is being done."

Jennifer said, "Try to visualize an organization in which, instead of all the employees going around trying to convince everyone else that they are right, everyone is seeking everyone else's point of view, hungering for different perspectives, and embracing diversity of thought; where open, honest dialogue is the norm. Sounds great, doesn't it?"

"I can't imagine what it would be like," Jerry said. "Is it like that at The Green Patch?"

"Not all the time, but just about," said Jennifer. "It's close enough that there is a significant discernible difference between the environment there and anyplace else I have ever been. It is the single greatest reason why generative learning is so prevalent there, why people's thought synergy produces so many new ideas and such rapid solutions to problems."

"Hold on, please!" Jerry almost shouted. "Thought synergy? Generative learning? What do these terms mean?"

"Sorry, Jerry," said Jennifer apologetically. "Thought synergy is about coming up with new ideas in a group situation. Someone mentions an idea and this sparks another idea in someone else, which goes on to spark more ideas. You've probably been in a situation with a few people in which you're trying to solve some problem or come up with a new idea. Someone mentions something, and this reminds you of a related thought. It works best when all participants are open and honest but no one is negative, making statements like 'That'll never work.' Generative learning is what you learn from these encounters. It's generative because it can exponentially produce new ideas and learning as you contribute different perspectives, much as a fire produces more heat, generates heat, as you throw on more fuel.

Jerry said, "I see. That helps, Jennifer. Thanks."

Jerry sat contemplating the information they had shared with him, and then he made some notes. Mary picked up the empty trays and headed to the kitchen while Jennifer and Natalie gazed at the fading light of the setting sun. When Jerry had finished writing, he looked up and said, "It makes sense to me. But how long does it take to transform a conventional organization into a learning organization?"

"It depends, Jerry," said Natalie. "It depends on how sincere management is about the change, and it depends how deep the scars are from the past. It also depends on how many employees are thinking tomatoes versus the other type. This is more about the journey than it is about arriving at a destination. Each step is progress. Although we are very open and honest at The Green Patch, there is room for improvement. When someone asks how long it will take, I always relate the story about the traveler who asked a farmer how long it would take to reach a certain destination. The farmer thought for a bit and then replied that he didn't know but if the traveler had left the day before, he might have arrived already."

"I see what you mean," Jerry said. "My guess is that Microprojects has a long journey ahead of it." After he made some more notes he looked up thoughtfully and said, "I need to be very careful about how I approach management. There are a lot of programs in place, sacred cows that management may worship. I'm not sure how to deal with it, but I need to be careful. I need to think about it more. I'm sure I'll need your help."

"You have the best feel for your management and the culture at Microprojects. After you have thought about it, feel free to bounce your ideas off any of us," Natalie volunteered.

"What's the next lesson?" he asked as Mary returned with a tray of something that looked like chocolate sweets and set it on the table.

"Well," Mary began, "the next lesson in organizational gardening might be called 'tilling and caring for the crops'. It's all about providing equal opportunities for all members of the organization and creating an environment where all are winners."

"Equal opportunities? What do you mean?" Jerry asked.

"OK, Jerry," Natalie said. "Let's say you were planting a field of corn, not a field of 'thinking corn,' by the way, just ordinary corn. Since it's not thinking, it's very dependent on you. One of the needs is nutrients. How would you, say, fertilize the field of corn?"

"Well, I would just fertilize the field," Jerry said, sounding confused.

"You mean you wouldn't fertilize certain corn stalks more or water them more or provide more sunlight for some than others?" Natalie asked.

"No, that would be ridiculous," Jerry responded. "Why give special treatment to certain stalks? You would end up limiting your crop."

"Exactly," Natalie said. "It's common sense, even for someone who claims to not have a green thumb. So if you had a group of employees, would you give some of them special treatment? Provide special opportunities for some that you wouldn't provide for others?"

"It sure doesn't seem like I should," Jerry said. "But, hey! I think I'm beginning to understand what you are getting at. At Microprojects, we have a lot of programs that tend to favor certain employees. But I have never thought about it in that light. It has always seemed to be the norm, even though the majority of the people tend to get upset; a lot more people are de-motivated than motivated."

"What you've described is typical of a lot of organizations," said Mary. "Programs such as pay for performance, employee-of-the-month or -year, or any program that ranks people based on a normal curve or instills competition between groups where there is interdependency tend to backfire and generate resentment. These programs are usually focused on the upper fifteen percent or so of the workforce. The purpose of course is to instill the drive that comes from competition. 'If you outperform the rest, then you will reap the rewards.' And it does motivate some people, but a lot of others realize there's a Catch 22; no matter how hard you try, the target has moved. Instead of it being a motivator, it becomes a de-motivator for the majority of the people. Instead of becoming energized, many feel victimized, and for good reason. It is the same as planting a field of corn and then fertilizing only fifteen percent of the crop or only certain stalks. That's ludicrous, but no more so than the programs a lot of organizations use to supposedly motivate their people. Unfortunately, this is also typical of the programs used in our public education systems. It says 'grade on the curve, or fertilize only fifteen percent, compete rather than cooperate. As one of the well-known organizational behaviorists says, 'Life is about getting A's, not some normal distribution curve.' Why not try to make everyone a winner? Create a system where everyone wins, and you will reap a full harvest, not just a partial one. Of course, even if the field is leveled, some people will still grow more, the same as some cornstalks grow taller even if they were all fertilized the same."

"I understand what you are saying, Mary, and I agree with you, but what kind of system can motivate everyone? Let's face it—some people do outperform others, and some do add more value. If they do, shouldn't they be fairly compensated?" asked Jerry.

"For sure," Mary responded, "But there must be clear expectations and a measurement system to determine if the expectations are being met."

"What do you mean?" Jerry asked.

"The whole idea of differentiating compensation based on contribution is a noble idea," Mary explained. "The problem is that very often what 'meeting or exceeding expectations' means is vague, as are the boundaries of a person's responsibility. The other problem is that the process for measuring whether a person meets or exceeds expectations is either nonexistent, vague, not understood, or based on the perception of management who judge performance based on sometimes-infrequent interactions with the people they are assessing. Let's look at these, one at a time. Jennifer . . ."

"You remember we talked about the importance of clear boundaries before," Jennifer began.

"Yes, I recall," said Jerry, "that it's very important to describe the boundaries of your responsibility very clearly, otherwise you do something you believe is within your jurisdiction and then get in trouble for it. After that, you may be very hesitant to take on other responsibilities for fear of getting clobbered again and may get labeled as a poor performer. Or you may act outside your area of competence and make a significant mistake, not because you are a poor performer but because the limits of your responsibility were not communicated. This is the reason I asked Blackburn specifically what I will be responsible for in my new role. I don't want to act outside of what he believes is my area of responsibility, nor do I want to do something that I don't have the skills to do."

"Exactly," said Natalie. "And a thinking tomato makes sure the boundaries are clear before it acts, and it obtains the skills it needs. You learn fast, Jerry. The next thing is to make sure that the expectations are very clear and that everyone understands exactly what good performance, poor performance, or excellent performance means. I don't mean by just labeling it something like 'exceeds job requirements'; I mean by specifically describing for a particular job the behavior, the progress, the goals, or the actions that must be accomplished. All of these, of course, must be measurable."

"I can see why all of that is important," Jerry said. "If I understand what I am responsible for and how my performance is measured, then it is up to me, provided of course I have the requisite knowledge and skills. And if the boundaries were correctly described, I would have the right knowledge and skills or at least be given the opportunity to get the right stuff."

"Right, Jerry," Mary said. "Now, the third part of the equation concerns who evaluates the performance. If the performance can be measured accurately, there isn't a problem. However, if you are talking about behaviors such as interpersonal skills, taking initiative, being energetic, being a good team player, or other 'soft' skills, it is a lot more difficult to assess. In this case it is best to rely on a lot of input from the people who actually interact with the person frequently, not some remote manager."

"Yeah," Jerry said. "Last year, during my performance review, Andy Mills said I wasn't a good team player but he didn't tell me why. I don't think he ever witnessed me firsthand in a team situation, so his evaluation must have been based on hearsay. I had had a disagreement with one of the other project managers who worked for Mills, and I think he blamed me for some problems with one of his projects. Don't think I'm feeling sorry for myself, but Mills never explained why I wasn't a good team player; he only said I should know what he was talking about. I brooded over it for several weeks, and when raise time came around, my increase was less than my peers, so I got angry about it again."

"That's typical," said Mary. "What we have been describing is a process for leveling the playing field so everyone has an equal opportunity. And if everyone performs as expected, then all of them should be rewarded, not just fifteen percent. If no one performs as expected, then no one should be rewarded. If some people rise higher than others, then they should be rewarded. But even if the playing field is leveled, differentiating on performance is a difficult thing to pull off without de-motivating some portion of those who aren't rewarded."

"So what's the alternative?" asked Jerry.

"Reward group, team, department, site, or company performance," Mary responded. "It still has to be based on specific goals, but it tends to be a lot less controversial than the alternative. This is the process we use at The Green Patch. If the company does well, everyone shares in the profits; if not, we should each blame the person looking back at us in the mirror. We don't pit one group against another either, because all of the groups and departments are so intertwined. Competition between groups, teams, or department almost never takes place at The Green Patch. We do, however, use a lot of peer recognition. In such cases, one's peers nominate him or her for an award because of an outstanding contribution to the team or department and the company. Usually, these awards are more authentic and more meaningful when they come from peers."

"I like the idea of peer recognition. But how about on the other end? What if some people aren't carrying their weight?" Jerry asked. "They get the reward even though they didn't perform. It doesn't seem right."

"We don't find that to be a problem," said Natalie. "If an organization provides the right learning environment, clear boundaries, clear expectations, and measures performance in a meaningful way, the problem you describe is minimal. Besides, one of the strongest forces in an organization is peer pressure. If someone isn't performing, it affects the whole company, like the proverbial bad apple. Peer pressure can be a lot more powerful that threats from management."

"Very interesting," said Jerry, "very interesting."

"And one last item," volunteered Natalie. "Be careful when you use symbols to motivate people. Very often the focus may be on the symbol rather than what it symbolizes."

"What do you mean?" asked Jerry.

"I'll give you an example," Natalie replied. "The bioscience company I worked at before had a program in place to supposedly empower teams and get them to be self directed. The company would award a large engraved glass trophy whenever a team reached a certain empowerment level based on an assessment of the team's performance. It was supposed to represent quite an achievement. Management stressed it so strongly that after a while the focus was more on getting the trophy than on the identity, behaviors, and skills of the team. Teams started just doing those things that would allow them to pass the assessment, checking off the items one, two, and three. The emblem became the objective, not the identity. But if you interacted with one of these 'empowered' teams, you realized that a lot of it was bogus. There was bickering, finger pointing, poor customer focus, and victimization, hardly the characteristics of a team that is empowered. But the problem was created by management, first because they stressed the emblem more than the behaviors, and second because the teams that had not received the trophy were made to feel there was something wrong with them. They didn't feel they had the time to make the journey, but the journey is where most of the learning takes place. Rather than the emblem being a byproduct of the program, it became the product. I've seen the same thing happen with titles and positions and awards. None of these should be the primary focus, and management can greatly influence this by what it stresses."

"I see what you mean," said Jerry. "The same thing has happened at Microprojects."

Jerry sat, making notes while Mary and Natalie cleared away the trays and glasses. He checked his watch and said, "This has been very helpful. I think I'm beginning to understand what it means to provide the right environment for people to thrive. Although it doesn't seem like it will necessarily be easy, it definitely is the right way to go."

"Neither was losing fifty pounds," Jennifer said as she put her hands around her waist. "But if your vision is strong enough, you can make it happen. I think Joe Blackburn and Microprojects are very fortunate to have you head up this change. And don't feel like you are alone. You can always come to any of us for help, advice, or just to kick ideas around."

"That's comforting to know," Jerry responded. "By the way, speaking of losing fifty pounds, would you like to go running together tomorrow evening? I've started getting back into my exercise program. It always helps to have someone pace you."

"Would love to," Jennifer said.

Jerry and Jennifer found Mary and Natalie cleaning up the dishes in the kitchen. Jerry gave both of them a big hug and thanked them for their help. He looked at Mary and told her that he appreciated her sharing her past with him. Of all the conversations they had had, this was one of the most significant. Jennifer walked him to his car. She said she was looking forward to their run. Jerry drove off feeling very satisfied and significantly better than when he had arrived.

Chapter Twenty

Learning about Learning

*T*he first thing Monday morning, Jerry contacted the woman who gave the seminars on accelerated learning. Her name was Gail Henderson. Mary said her office was in Oakland and the name of her company was Enlightenment, Inc. Gail answered the phone, and Jerry explained that Mary Green had recommended her. He briefly explained what he was trying to do at Microprojects. Gail agreed that the course would be of considerable help to him. She said he was fortunate because she would be conducting a session the following week and that he was more than welcome to join the class. She said the seminar would be held in Marin County, just outside the town of Mill Valley. She advised him to stay at the conference facility because several nights they would be working late.

That evening Jerry went running with Jennifer. Jerry told her that he had lucked out and would be able to attend the class the following week. Jennifer said that she had taken the same class the previous year because one of her roles at The Green Patch was conducting learning sessions. She told Jerry he was in for a unique learning experience. He tried to get her to give him details, but she said that he should be patient and that any description of what was to take place would not do justice to the actual experience.

Jerry spent the rest of the week making rough plans for how he would fill his new role. He realized he still had one heck of a lot to learn about facilitating change at Microprojects because the existing culture was so ingrained. At times he would think that it was just too big a task, and he would start to worry. Each time he would catch himself and realize, *All I'm doing is giving myself negative feedback that is programming my subconscious to fail.* He also recalled that negativity was one of his main core opportunities, and it would take a strong self awareness to change this habit. To control these destructive feelings he purposely started thinking about all he had going for himself. Jerry had Mary, Natalie, and Jennifer to help him. He decided to make an appointment with Mary to witness firsthand some of the things that were going on at The Green Patch. He called her and she readily agreed to his visit, so he scheduled a whole day later in the week to go there and observe. But he needed something else. Wouldn't it be great if he could work directly with someone who already understood the process? Unfortunately there was no one at Microprojects who could even mentor him, much less assist him. Otherwise Blackburn might have asked them to head up the effort. Then he recalled something Jennifer had said to him about one of her roles at The Green Patch being facilitation. *I wonder,* Jerry thought. *I just wonder . . .*

The accelerated learning class was scheduled to start at 4:00 on Sunday afternoon. Gail said it was an odd time to start a class, but this way no one would have to fight the Bay Area traffic, and besides, there were a lot of things about the class that one might call *odd.* Jerry drove across the Golden Gate Bridge just after 1:00. It was one of those perfect spring days in the Bay Area. The sky, the bay, and the ocean were all a deep, endless blue. Hundreds of sailboats dotted the bay with their big white sails unfurled and wakes of white foam streaming behind. A sense of pleasant anticipation overtook Jerry as he drove up Highway 101 toward Mill Valley.

The conference center was located among a large grove of redwood trees. The modern structure blended well with the natural surroundings. Jerry registered at the desk and put his things in his room. He made sure he knew where the conference room was located and then spent the next hour walking the grounds of the center. At a quarter to four, he entered the conference room. There were seven or eight people already in the room, conversing. Jerry was immediately taken aback by the way the room was arranged. Instead of the typical U-shaped seating arrangement or lecture-type setup used so often in classes at Microprojects, there were fifteen or so seats arranged in a circle. The walls were adorned with various colorful posters and charts that would evidently be used to reinforce various parts of the class. Several round tables were located around the perimeter of the room, which looked out through large picture windows onto the grounds of the conference center. Classical music was playing in the background.

A woman who looked to be in her late thirties or early forties walked over, reached out her hand, and said, "Hello, I'm Gail Henderson. Welcome to the conference." Jerry was struck by how much she reminded him of Mary. He immediately took a liking to her. She had a certain confidence and openness about her.

"I'm Jerry Artson. It's a real pleasure to be here. I was just marveling at the way you have the room arranged; not exactly what I expected. Mary told me it would be different."

"Thanks. All the arrangements have a purpose, and you'll understand more as we get into the program," Gail responded. "I'm very glad you could make it. Let me get your name tag and introduce you to the rest of the participants."

By 4:00, all of the participants had arrived. Most were from the Bay Area or Southern California, but a few were from the East Coast or the Midwest. Ages ranged from young to old. Jerry immediately felt very relaxed with these people. He felt he had known them a lot longer than ten minutes.

Gail asked everyone to take a seat in the circle. She briefly told them about some housekeeping items and then explained that participants usually bring more than their bodies to these seminars; that in addition to turning off their pagers and cell phones, they should consider getting rid of some other things. She went on to explain that some of the 'baggage' included worries, anticipations, plans, 'to do's,' and so on. So the first thing they would do was to become centered. The purpose of centering was to focus on being physically and mentally present. She asked each person to close his or her eyes to attempt to stop or at least slow down the internal dialogue, the voice inside their heads that was always silently chattering about this or that. It was easier, she said, to stop our internal dialogue if we shut off outside sensory stimulation. As she put on a somewhat familiar "new age" piano solo, she explained that the only sensory stimulation should be the music. Jerry looked around at the other participants and closed his eyes. At first he felt a little silly and odd; you don't usually close your eyes fifteen minutes after being introduced to a new group of people. Jerry found it difficult to stop his internal dialogue, and he imagined others shared his discomfort. Gail must have sensed their uneasiness. She softly said that they must not force their internal dialogue to stop but let their thoughts come and go and not dwell or hang on to them.

Gradually his uneasiness abated, and he found himself not thinking but flowing with the music. For some reason closing his eyes made him recall a time several years before when he was with his two brothers and sister-in-law. They were drinking champagne and eating caviar. There were two kinds of caviar, red and black. His brothers had asked him to shut his eyes and see if he could tell the difference between the red and black. He didn't recall whether he was able to or not, but now, thinking about it, he was overcome with a heightened feeling of appreciation for times such as that. He saw his brothers only a few times a year, and this particular occasion had stuck in his mind. He became so engrossed in the memory that it nearly brought tears to his eyes, and he almost totally forgot where he was until Gail softly said, "Now, please open your eyes."

Only three or four minutes had passed, but it had seemed much longer. Jerry felt completely relaxed and contented. As he looked around at the other participants, he noticed that they also appeared calm, even refreshed. Gail asked each of them to answer a couple of questions: "Why are you here?" and "What do you hope to take away from the experience?" Jerry noted that she now referred to the class as an experience and not a class. She asked everyone to give a little background on himself or herself and assured them there was no rush; they could speak whenever they so desired.

Jerry asked himself, *Why am I here?* He realized that there were several reasons; one was because it was going to be a unique experience, perhaps significantly different from any other he had had. He had not started out with this expectation, except maybe subconsciously, but since driving across the Golden Gate Bridge earlier in the day, he had become increasingly conscious of the value of a new experience and the pleasure the anticipation of something special brings. Another reason he was here was to learn more about accelerated learning. Most of his past experiences with learning had been negative. The very idea that learning could be positive and fun was very novel and fascinating. He felt like he was getting ready to drink from some special magic potion. The third reason, and oddly enough the least important at the moment, was that he anticipated that the experience would prepare him to better fulfill his new role at Microprojects.

They went around the circle, each person explaining his or her reasons. Many were similar to Jerry's. The backgrounds of the people ranged from corporate executive to training professional to people with their own consulting businesses. He felt he was part of an encounter group rather than a class. As Jerry explained his reasons, he felt as though he were talking to a group of close friends; each seemed keenly interested in what he had to say.

After the introductions, Gail laid out where they would be going and what they would be doing. It wasn't your ordinary run-of-the-mill agenda, typically done on a PowerPoint presentation with bullet points. She used three-dimensional figures and colorful charts with more pictures than words to describe what she called "our journey." She said that her role was that of a tour guide.

Over the next five days the class journeyed to places Jerry had never been. Gail explained, or rather demonstrated, that the roots of accelerated learning were in something she called *suggestopedia*, first developed by a Bulgarian doctor, Georgi Lozanov, in Sofia in the '60s. Lozanov's ideas were based on the power of suggestion in teaching or facilitating. She said that he believed that when the suggestion is that learning will be fun and easy rather than difficult, there is a much greater likelihood that people can learn. As she demonstrated this idea, Jerry recalled the comment that Natalie had made several weeks ago about the power of belief in yourself.

Gail demonstrated using three-dimensional models the five pillars of accelerated learning: *playing, music, relaxed mental states, pleasing views,* and *the role of the facilitator.*

Playing involves the use of games and a variety of fun exercises. Music is used as an integrated activity that can accelerate the learning of a particular subject matter. It is not about just playing music but is based on a more scientific rationale that certain types of music help reinforce learning during each stage of the learning process. The relaxed mental states are similar to the atmosphere of meditation that Gail placed the class in during the first few minutes of the experience and at various times throughout the five days. The pleasing views abounded, from the ambiance of the room to the colorful charts and posters to the views outside of redwoods through the large picture window. And Gail's facilitation skills were the glue that bound everything together. She seemed to always be aware of how each person was reacting, knowing when to slow down or move on, or when to pull something new from her seemingly endless inventory of games and activities.

Another important key learning that Gail demonstrated was the learning cycle. She described the five phases of the learning cycle, and the way the class was delivered was based on them. The first was the centering activity they had experienced at the beginning of the first day and again at the start of each successive day. The second phase she called the motivation phase. This is like the appetizers served before a meal that causes one to anticipate the food to come with a keen appetite. The third phase is the "aha" or discovery phase. Discovery is most effective when it is done by the individual or group rather than being explicitly force-fed by the facilitator. The fourth phase is the practice phase, in which the learning is solidified. And the last, or fifth phase, is the integration phase, in which we digest what we have learned and determine how we will make it a part of our being.

Gail also described a model that was familiar to Jerry. It was part of the memorable experience that Jerry had that day with Jennifer when she described the power of vision and the Seven P's. Gail produced a three-dimensional cardboard pyramid composed of five levels that she revealed one at a time. Jerry saw that she was not only teaching them a new concept but she was demonstrating the motivation phase that she had described previously. One could not help but be curious about what was written inside each of the five levels because they were initially hidden. Here was the learning pyramid in three dimensions like the one Jennifer had sketched for him at his house.

When Friday rolled around, Jerry could not believe how fast the week had gone. They had many different experiences. At one point she had the whole class dancing a Jewish wedding dance in a circle. At first Jerry thought it was stupid and he was a little embarrassed, but as he got into the dance, all of his inhibitions quickly disappeared. Now if he could only reproduce something similar to what he had experienced this week at Microprojects. As the group said their good-byes, Jerry's eyes began to water. This was such a beautiful experience that it was difficult to leave those with whom he had shared it. All committed to keep in touch and share their experiences in applying what they had learned.

As Jerry drove back across the Golden Gate Bridge, he felt he had been gone longer than a week. He hoped that this famous bridge was not some line of demarcation between imagination and reality, and he hoped he would retain the feeling he had experienced and the knowledge he had gained at this marvelous encounter in Mill Valley.

Chapter Twenty-One

A Partnership Blooms

*T*hroughout the accelerated learning experience in Mill Valley, Jerry had been considering something that would greatly improve the learning sessions he would be planning at Microprojects. He knew that Jennifer had taken the same accelerated learning class, and he knew that she applied what she knew routinely at The Green Patch. What if Jennifer would agree to co-facilitate with him? Wouldn't that be perfect?! But before he asked her, he needed to consult with Mary. Jerry knew he had the freedom to use whomever he needed; Blackburn had granted him that. He called Mary and asked if he could meet with her privately. He said he had a special favor to ask of her. Mary said to come by the nursery early Saturday morning.

Jerry arrived Saturday and walked to the back of the nursery where the roses were kept and where Mary could normally be found. As he approached the area he saw no one at first, then he noticed Mary sitting on a bench by the roses, seemingly gazing off in the distance. Her back was turned to him. The early morning sun and the beautiful colors gave the scene a mystical aura. He sensed that she might be in deep thought so he approached very quietly, stopping about fifteen feet from the bench. He continued to gaze at her and the scene around her for what seemed like a long time but what was probably only a few minutes or so; time seemed to stand still. Eventually, Mary must have sensed she was being watched because she slowly turned around and said, "Oh, hello Jerry. Sorry, I didn't hear you."

She silently gazed at the flowers for a few more moments and said, "I often come here and frequently become so mesmerized by the colors and forms, particularly when the roses are in full bloom and the sun is rising in the morning sky, like it is now. It's so easy to turn off my internal dialogue when I look at something so beautiful, so relaxing. I can truly 'stop the world.' You know, Jerry, I have a theory that breathing the perfume of roses is very healthful, although I have nothing to corroborate it, except that whenever I come here or visit my garden at home, I have a feeling of well-being and an increased sense of clarity. The smell reminds me, somehow, of my childhood. My mother always had roses, old roses, lots of them. They grew everywhere, and each season some more would be created by the cross fertilization of some of the previous season's plants. None of them had a special name, like these here, but it didn't matter. All went by the name "Rose." In the spring it was absolutely beautiful, breathtakingly beautiful. The most magical part was the smell, and it has been implanted so solidly in my memory that when I smell a rose, a part of me is always taken back to that time."

Again, she gazed at the scene around her. "My mother always had an uncanny ability to grow things. I think her main pleasure in life was gardening. There was a gardening club in the neighborhood, but mother never cared about joining. She said the only thing they did was gossip, and she had no interest in that. The club used to give a prize each month to the 'garden of the month' for the most beautiful yard. One month, mother's yard got it even though she wasn't a member. People used to come from all over to see her garden. They would ask her how she grew this or that, but she never knew; the only answer I ever heard her give was that 'you love them' and you will know how. I think it is from her I have taken my love for gardening. I can't imagine anything that gives such lasting pleasure. But here I am rambling on and on. How are you doing, Jerry? I recall you saying on the phone that you had something important to ask me."

Jerry, not ready to leave the moment and not sure yet how to ask Mary about Jennifer, said, "No problem, Mary. I'm doing fine. I was taken in by the view myself. You have so many flowers at the nursery and at your home, but you seem to spend more time with the roses. Now I see why. They must be your favorite flower."

"Yes, I think the rose is my favorite flower; so full of contradictions—beautiful inviting flowers and foliage but threatening thorns. It often reminds me of how so many people act, with their dichotomies of contradictory behaviors. Actually, it's not *the* favorite; it has a partner. Lavender is my other favorite. The two are such opposites they make excellent mates. They are beautiful grown together. The rose has so much depth, so much brilliance; it's an amazing teacher. Sit down with a rose and understand the world. But there's another side to it, too. It can be so stand-offish. It says 'Keep your distance, don't touch me, I can hurt, and I'm helpless at times, so take care of me, check on me, prune me, spray me, water me, and be patient, for sometimes I have fits. I might catch something going around, and when I do, I like to shrivel and wilt and spread it around—no point going it alone. Make sure you keep those little sticky flying pests off my buds. You know, the ones the ants like to nurture as if they were pets. Yuk! Ignore me and one day I might just commit suicide by attracting one of those underground rats.' Know any people who act like that, Jerry?"

Jerry was amused by Mary's description. She continued, "Such behaviors to endure from someone who is a *friend.* But it is all worth it and more, because what we see most of the time is a sight that has few equals. The flowers and the foliage. The flower—few words do it justice. The foliage starts brownish red, sometimes even purple, and slowly, patiently turns green. And oh, what greens! Here also I am lost for words. How to describe a rose? Think about a rainbow, borrow any shade or hue, take form to infinity, adopt shocking beauty, and while you're at it, emit an aroma that the nose knows and wants to know more, the sweetest of perfumes. Strange, isn't it, to pick a friend like lavender; so easy to have around. It says 'Don't worry about me; I can take care of myself. Give me some water if it is dry too long; even then I'll stay around. Save all that stuff you have and do for Madame Rose. Relax and enjoy me; my flowers are unique, with fewer colors than Madame R, ones she normally doesn't have: purples, blues, wine, sometimes green, and no similarity in shape to hers. Smell me; my odor is not only in my flowers but also in my leaves, my stems. It'll stay around for a long while; permanence is my creed. I rarely disappoint. If you like, wallow in me and then we'll smell the same. But, beware of the bees!' So I like them both and many other plants, of course. I have a special fondness for the rose, but she needs much more of my time."

"I'll consider planting some lavender. I didn't know they were so easy."

"After they are established, they immolate the thinking tomato; they need almost no care," she said. "Oh, by the way, how did your class go last week?"

"It was the most amazing learning experience I've ever had," Jerry exclaimed. "I'm still on a high!"

"I can see why, Jerry. Gail Henderson is a special person, and she is very adept at delivering her class in a way that reinforces what she is teaching. I've known Gail for years. After Natalie came here and introduced the idea of organizational gardening, we both attended Gail's class. It has helped us enormously as we delivered the message to all of the employees here."

"And I understand that Jennifer has taken the class, too," Jerry stammered, not knowing where or how to begin to ask what he came for.

Mary gazed at the grin on Jerry's face. Sometimes it was so easy to read what he was thinking. "Is that the important thing you have on your mind? So you'd like to have Jennifer help you at Microprojects? Is that it?" Mary replied with a knowing smile and a twinkle in her eye.

Totally surprised, Jerry asked, "But how did you know?"

"Oh, just intuition," Mary said. "And, besides, Jennifer suggested it the other day. She asked me if she could help you out. She said that it would be easier if you worked with someone who was experienced with the process. She also admitted she was looking for a new challenge."

"She did?" Jerry asked. "But are you sure you can do without her?" he asked anxiously.

"No problem," Mary said. "It is entirely up to her. But I think that she expects to be paid, and I don't think she comes cheap. She is also very adept at curriculum design, and that will be a big help as you put your course together. I'm sure she will be able to borrow some of the processes we've used here."

"Great," Jerry said. "Is she working today? I can't wait to talk to her."

"No; she's off today," Mary responded. "But you can probably catch her at the house."

Jerry drove out to Mary's house and found Jennifer working in the back yard. "Hey, Jennifer," Jerry called as he spotted her on her knees by a flowerbed.

"Hi Jerry! What's up?" Jennifer asked, surprised to see him. "How did the class go last week?"

"It was everything you said and more," Jerry said excitedly. "Definitely the best learning experience I've ever had."

"And when you think what the world would be like if every learning experience was even close to that . . ." Jennifer said. "Do you think you can create the same experience for the people at Microprojects?"

"With a little bit of help," Jerry said slyly. "Yes, I have been looking around for some help," he said as he scanned the grounds as if searching for an answer in the flowerbeds.

"What kind of help are you looking for?" she asked innocently.

"Oh, maybe someone who understands and has practiced accelerating learning; someone who understands organizational gardening and self-cultivation; someone who thinks like a tomato. Do you know anyone like that?" he asked, smiling.

"Oh, Jerry," she exclaimed as she gave him a big hug. "You've been talking to Mary, haven't you? And here you've been leading me on. Of course I know someone."

"And someone cheap," he added.

"Well, keep looking," she said as she faked a pout.

"Seriously," Jerry asked anxiously. "Would you be willing to work with me? The two of us could change Microprojects overnight!"

"It might take a *little* more time than that. Patience, remember?" she asked. "Yes, I'd love to work with you. I've already gotten Mary's permission to take a leave. I know that sounds presumptuous, but I was going to ask *you* if you needed any help, so I wanted to check it out with Mary before. When can we start?"

"I've one small hurdle to overcome before I can commit to contracting your services," he said. "I've a meeting with Blackburn on Monday to give him a status report. I'll need to make sure he concurs with my plans, but I don't expect him to object. He has pretty much given me free rein and a decent budget to do this any way I please. Now that I will have you to work with me, I am confident we can pull it off, although I know there's a mountain of work ahead of us."

"You're right about the mountain of work, but the subjects we will be teaching are *about* moving mountains. I'm confident we will succeed. I can hardly wait to get started," she said as she dug into the flowerbed with her trowel.

Monday morning Jerry walked up to Joe's office. Anita Evans smiled and motioned him in. As he entered, Joe extended his hand. "Good to see you, Jerry. I've been looking forward to this update. Tell me what you've got going."

Jerry filled him in on what he had learned since their last meeting two weeks earlier. He related his experience at the accelerated learning class. He said that he was still working on the details for the pilot session they would have with Joe's managers but that there would probably be two parts; the first half would focus on self-cultivation and the second half on organizational gardening. Jerry said that he would like to contract with someone to help him, someone who had experienced the processes firsthand and who was also an accomplished facilitator. Joe sat, listening and smiling and nodding in agreement as Jerry talked. Joe said it was up to Jerry. The budget they had agreed on was healthy enough to cover a consultant with no problem if he wanted one. Joe said he looked forward to hearing more of the details in a couple of weeks. Jerry thanked him profusely and almost gave him a hug as he walked from the room. Joe smiled to himself as Jerry left. He knew his hunch had been right about this young man.

Jerry raced back to his office, called the nursery, and asked for Jennifer. When she answered the phone, he said that it was a go. They could start as soon as she could make herself available. He would look for an office for her and work with purchasing to draw up a contract for her services. Jennifer said she would be there on

Thursday. As he hung up the phone, he realized she hadn't even asked him what her fee would be. She seemed as excited as he was, and clearly it wasn't about money.

Chapter Twenty-Two

The Plan Is Approved

J ennifer moved into an office several doors down from Jerry's. Numerous whispers raced along the grapevine over this development, but Jennifer and Jerry had no time to worry about what people thought. They worked twelve-hour days putting the proposal together for the four-day learning session. Jerry felt fairly confident that Blackburn would approve their proposal, but they also needed to review it with Microprojects' CEO, Jim Crabtree.

Jerry was amazed how easy it was to work with Jennifer. As Jerry described the culture at Microprojects, Jennifer recommended interventions that would provide the greatest leverage toward bringing about change. They decided that the greatest problems at Microprojects were the infection of victimization and the lack of trust caused by the downsizing and the past command-and-control culture; it was all-pervasive. Nobody wanted to take responsibility for anything, and finger pointing was rampant. This was probably the result of the previous strong command-and-control environment and the lack of a plan to change the culture once Blackburn had taken over as division manager.

After a lot of discussion, they decided to propose a two-day focus on self-cultivation with a follow-up two-day session on organizational gardening for the pilot session with the managers. Strangely enough, the denial behavior was greatest with Blackburn's staff, perhaps because they didn't want to believe that anything had really changed and that they had lost power. Until they started behaving proactively, it was unrealistic to expect the rest of the company to change.

Jerry and Jennifer completed the proposal with time to spare. It was Wednesday, and Jerry didn't have to review the proposal with Blackburn until the following Monday. Jennifer had several loose ends she needed to tie up at the nursery, and Jerry needed to think about the best way of presenting the proposal to Blackburn. Jerry also had several questions he needed to answer about the projects he had transferred to other engineers. Jerry and Jennifer agreed to touch base on Monday after he had reviewed the proposal with Joe.

Jerry was looking forward to reviewing the proposal as he arrived at Joe's office on Monday morning. They discussed the proposed four-day class until about noon. Jerry went through the entire program from start to finish. He described the major changes that had to take place for Microprojects' culture transition. Joe asked a lot of questions, but he didn't change anything. They were scheduled to review it with Jim Crabtree in two weeks. Joe said that some of the modifications Jerry recommended were counter to practices Crabtree had put in place years before. He didn't know how Jim would react to Jerry's recommendations, but Jerry should be ready to defend his position. Joe indicated that potentially the most sensitive area would be the proposed changes in the incentive-pay arena. He also indicated that Jim might not understand the idea that Microprojects could ever neglect the needs of its employees. In addition, he might be uneasy about giving everyone so much responsibility and authority. Jerry should also be prepared to justify the costs of the new programs. Joe indicated he would be available to help Jerry if needed and to feel free to contact him at any time. Jerry thanked Joe for the heads up and his offer and said he would be ready.

Stabs of doubt battered Jerry's brain as he thought about his upcoming encounter with Crabtree. Jim was, after all, the person who had built Microprojects from a small backroom company into a multimillion dollar corporation that employed several thousand people. Who was Jerry to tell him how to run his company? Jerry discussed his doubts with Jennifer; she laughed and said he was just up to his old courtship with negativity again. Jennifer reminded him that he had seen firsthand the benefit of culture change at The Green Patch. This proposal could transform the culture of Microprojects. He had the backing of Blackburn, and Joe wouldn't throw him into the lion's den if he hadn't thought that Jerry was on the right track. Jerry should approach this meeting with Crabtree with the same positive attitude he had at his first meeting with Blackburn several months earlier. Jerry knew she was right, and he worked at getting his attitude adjusted and seeing himself in a positive light.

At last the day of reckoning arrived. Jerry had gotten over his self doubt and was looking forward to the meeting. He walked into Joe's office at the scheduled time. He had never met Crabtree before. He was at least six foot two and dressed in a dark pinstriped business suit. He had a presence about him like he was used to people deferring to him. After introductions were made, Jim said, "Joe has spoken very highly of you, Jerry. He says that in order to survive in this new millennium, we need to make some significant changes to our company, and you have a plan. I'm looking forward to what you have to say."

Jerry nervously responded, "I, I . . . appreciate the opportunity to share my ideas with you, sir."

Jerry then described what he had reviewed with Joe two weeks earlier. Crabtree sat stone-faced through the whole spiel while Joe sat with a confident smile on his face, nodding in agreement as Jerry went along. Jerry couldn't tell whether Crabtree was angry or indifferent or pleased. *He must be one heck of a poker player,* Jerry thought. When Jerry finished, Crabtree sat staring at him for what seemed like an eternity, and then he spoke. "Joe has told me he's proposed a budget of two hundred thousand dollars for the development and implementation of this training. With the time people will spend away from work, it will cost a lot more than that. What's the payback?"

Jerry thought for a few moments and said, "Ultimately, greater knowledge and skills throughout the organization, fewer levels of management, better communications, and, most important, the employees interfacing with the customers will be empowered to act, which ultimately will result in more satisfied customers and more business. I can't give you an exact figure, but I just know it's huge. Besides, sir, what do you figure 'victimization' alone costs Microprojects in just a year?"

Crabtree looked intently at Jerry as if he had just switched his brain into "calculation" mode. Slowly nodding his head he responded, "Millions of dollars, Jerry, millions of dollars." Then he looked very seriously at Jerry again and said, "We've depended on our incentive-pay system since the company began, and you're proposing we change it? And our employee-of-the-year program was something I personally started. Why, Joe here was one of the first recipients. How could you ever think of doing away with them?"

Jerry had thought about his response for several days and said, "Mr. Crabtree, you and Mr. Blackburn are exceptional individuals. How would it be if everyone in the company came even close to being as sharp as the two of you?"

"Why, nothing could stop us," Crabtree responded, looking over at Joe, a little jokingly but pleased that Jerry appreciated their worth.

"Then how could you ever expect to achieve such a state if you nurture only a small fraction of your workforce?" Jerry asked.

Blackburn smiled as Crabtree sat in silence for what seemed like another eternity. Jerry wondered if he had gone too far. Finally, Jim began to smile also and said, "You're absolutely right, son, you're absolutely right. Obviously, you have thought about this a lot."

He reached out and grabbed Jerry's hand and shook it. With a smile and an expression of warmth that surprised Jerry he said, "Jerry, it is no secret that I have been grooming Joe here to take my place as CEO. Heck, I'm ready to retire and take it easy and let Joe and the rest of you grow my stock in the company. Ethel and I have seven grandchildren. I never spent enough time with my daughter or my son, or Ethel, for that matter. Maybe I can pay back a small amount of the debt by at least letting the grandkids know who their granddad is as Ethel and I go through our golden years. And I've always been an avid sailor, which might come from the time I spent in the Navy. I've wanted to take a long sailing voyage but never had the time. If I don't do it soon, I'll be too old. So the time is right for me to give up the helm here. I built this company from scratch, but I think Joe and some of you youngsters have a better feel for how to navigate this ship through the choppy waters of this new millennium. The thing I have always marveled about Joe, in addition to his intellect and technical expertise, is his intuition, his raw, gut feeling about people . . . it's uncanny! In the twenty-plus years he's worked for me, I have never known him to be wrong about a major direction the company should take, and I doubt this will be any different. Have at it, son. I like your spunk and energy. You have my blessings and my backing. Good luck to you, and if I can do anything to help, you let me know!"

And that's how the major changes at Microprojects were blessed.

Chapter Twenty-Three

The Pilot Class

*J*erry stopped by Jennifer's office right after his meeting with Crabtree and Blackburn. When Jennifer looked up from her computer, Jerry gave her a thumbs up, and she broke into a big smile. "I knew you wouldn't have any problem," she told Jerry gleefully.

"No, he didn't have but a few questions, but those were some zingers. I got the impression he was pretty much convinced already. Evidently he has a lot of confidence in Blackburn because he mentioned that Joe is next in line for CEO. I don't think that's public knowledge yet, although Gene Larson has had it on his radar screen for some time."

"Good choice," Jennifer commented. "I'm very impressed with Joe also. He stopped by the other day and introduced himself. We talked, or rather I talked for twenty minutes or so. He seemed very interested in what I was doing. Or maybe he was just checking me out to see what kind of consultant you hired."

"Or maybe he was 'checking you out.' " Jerry replied. "You know Joe isn't married, don't you?"

"No, Jerry, I wasn't aware," Jennifer said haltingly. "Glad you told me. He would be a real find for some woman. The man has a certain presence and charisma about him. In many ways he reminds me of Mary. I can't understand why you used to dislike him so much."

"Actually, when I disliked him I hadn't really ever met him; I'd just pass him in the hall. I based my impression on hearsay. It just goes to show you how wrong we can be about people and how erroneous our mental models can be."

"Yep," Jennifer replied. "It just shows you. Now back to work. I think I have the design for the class pretty much complete. You have time to go over it?"

"Sure," Jerry said. "Let me grab a cup of coffee and I'll be right back. Can I get you one?"

"No thanks. I had a cup at my favorite coffee shop on the way to work this morning. Besides, the coffee they serve around here could dissolve your insides. Maybe the problem with the culture at Microprojects is really caused by the coffee everyone drinks," Jennifer said, laughing.

"Could be," Jerry agreed. "All of this work for nothing! Be right back."

Blackburn had told Jerry that they should shoot for the end of May, about two weeks away, for the pilot session. Joe felt that it was best to expose all of the upper-level managers first and have them critique the course before they rolled it out to the entire site. Joe somewhat surprised Jerry by saying he would also be taking part in the pilot group.

Jerry and Jennifer reviewed the curriculum design she had put together one last time, making some minor adjustments. With two weeks to go before the class started, the participant manuals needed to be printed and several charts and props put together, and time was running out. Jerry needed to finalize the reservations for a conference room and make other logistics arrangements. They decided it was best to have the conference off-site. This way, people would be less likely to be distracted or tempted to rush back to their offices to check their phone or e-mail every time there was a break. The place they had chosen was right on the coast, just south of Carmel in the Big Sur area, and it offered a very relaxed and picturesque setting.

The two weeks flew by. Suddenly it was Friday, and the class was to begin on Monday. Jerry was in the office, picking up a few things before he and Jennifer drove down to Big Sur to set up the conference room. Jerry was walking down the hall when he ran into Gene Larson. Jerry hadn't talked to Gene in weeks. It seemed that since his promotion, all of his work friends were hesitant to associate with him, or maybe they were afraid to because of the perceived class structure at Microprojects. Jerry hoped that would soon change.

"Hi, Gene! How's it going?" Jerry asked. "Where have you been hiding?"

"Oh hello, Jer" Gene said meekly. "Or should I be saying 'Mr. Artson'. "

"No—'Jerry' will do fine, Gene." Jerry said, feeling a little peculiar. "I'm no different than before. Besides, I miss our discussions, although I have been so busy I have hardly had time to miss anything."

"I hear all of the managers are going down to Big Sur for some class you're putting on. Rumor has it that they will all get shock treatments; that's about the only management training they can understand."

That's the old Gene, Jerry thought. "Well, whatever it is, we're going to try it out on them and then dish it out to everyone, so you better hope it's not too painful or distasteful."

"Well, if nothing else, you'll keep them out of our hair for a while. Tell you what, Jer. Why don't you lock 'em all up down there for six months or so? Give them all their telephones and computers but don't connect them to the outside world. Let them blather on at their big meetings and make their big plans but keep it within the confines of the building. I guarantee you that within six weeks the profits here will double. Just remember, it was my suggestion. You can put me in for that employee-of-the-year award for thinking of it."

"I think we may be eliminating the employee-of-the-year award, Gene," Jerry said. "You just missed it."

"No employee-of-the-year award?" Gene said, grabbing his heart, feigning disappointment. "What on earth is going to keep me motivated all year?"

"They're replacing it with 'joker of the year,' and you should be a shoo-in for that one, Gene," Jerry said, laughing. "I've got to run. Catch you in a couple of weeks. Don't party too hard while the 'cats' are away."

Sunday, Jerry picked Jennifer up at Mary's, and they drove to the conference center to set up the room. When they finished, it resembled the room at the accelerated learning session in Mill Valley. Rather than a circular-chair arrangement, they would be using circular tables, five tables with five participants at each. They expected all of the managers to show up. Blackburn had sent out a note saying he expected everyone to attend. It was a command performance, and no one would refuse.

Sunday night, Jennifer and Jerry had dinner at a quaint little French restaurant in Carmel. They toasted the success of the session. They turned in early, but Jerry was so excited that he had a hard time going to sleep. All the weeks of preparation were finally coming to fruition. He considered phoning Jennifer to review a couple of details but thought better of it; better to give their minds a rest and get a good night's sleep.

Monday morning, Jerry and Jennifer arrived at the room early to make some last-minute preparations and to greet the participants as they arrived. Jerry knew most of the managers' names, but he had met only a few of them even though he was part of the staff. He had been so busy he hadn't had time to get to know them. He wasn't sure what they thought of him or how they would react to what he and Jennifer would say. This caused him to feel a little unsure of himself. He countered his feeling of doubt with his strong belief in the material he would be suggesting, and the knowledge that Blackburn and Crabtree supported him dispelled the doubts. He was particularly glad that Blackburn had decided to participate.

Jennifer and Jerry had placed name tents on the tables so everyone would know where to sit. Jerry felt that otherwise there would probably be twenty-four managers vying to sit at Blackburn's table so they could suck up. Actually, Jerry exaggerated, but some of the managers would leap at the opportunity, particularly Jerry's ex-boss, Andy Mills.

The session started with some opening remarks from Blackburn. He introduced Jennifer and Jerry and gave some information on their backgrounds. He thanked everyone for coming and said they were in for a unique learning experience that would lay the foundation for a much-needed change in the culture at Microprojects as the company transformed itself to an empowered organization. The program had his full support, but he was open to input from the staff as to how it could be improved or changed. He also said that for the next five days they should think of him as just another participant and not the division manager. He then turned the session over to Jennifer and took his seat.

Jennifer told the group that the first thing they were going to do was rid themselves of extra baggage by becoming centered. She said that centering was about becoming focused, shutting off internal dialogue, and being physically and mentally present rather than mentally somewhere else. As she explained the process, Mills whispered something to Craig Wilson, the purchasing manager, who was sitting beside him. Craig laughed and whispered something back. She said that she was going to play a piece of music, *Elegia,* by Karl Jenkins. She said that to her, the music evoked a feeling of hope and that it should set the mood for what the conference was about. She then started the music. Andy snickered and nudged Craig again, and both laughed and turned to see what Blackburn was doing. Joe, eyes closed, seemed to be lost in a trance. Both Mills and Wilson wiped the smiles off their faces and closed their eyes.

As the music ended, Jennifer said softly that everyone should open his or her eyes. She brought out a large three-dimensional pyramid that represented the learning pyramid but had all the names of the levels turned inside-out except the bottom one on which was written the word *environment* in gold letters. She asked them to discuss at their tables the following question, written on a flip chart. It read: *Are we able to create our environment or does our environment create us?*

Andy Mills raised his hand and said that he didn't understand the question and asked Jennifer to explain it more. She said that by environment she meant who we are, where we work, what we do, essentially everything in our personal and professional lives. She said that the question was asking whether we can change these things or are we at the mercy of them. He asked if she could tell him more, but she said that they should try to answer the question with the information she had given them, that if she told them any more, it might inappropriately influence their opinions.

The conversation started slowly but gradually took on more energy. After about twenty minutes, Jennifer asked them to stop and share what they had discussed. No one said anything. It seemed that all were waiting for Blackburn to speak. He said nothing.

After a very long, pregnant pause, Jack Crenshaw raised his hand and said, "I think our environment determines us. We are all a function of our parents' genetic pool, our upbringing, and what goes on around us. That's just the way it is."

Mills joined in. "I agree. You either get the breaks or you don't; you've got the brains or you don't; not a lot you can do about it one way or the other. Know what I mean?"

Anita Hurtado, one of three women on Blackburn's staff, raised her hand and said, "I think both are true. Environment has a lot to do with it, but you can change it, too."

Several hands shot up, and several people started talking at once. Jennifer quietly but sternly broke in and said, "OK. One of the ground rules is that only one person speaks at a time. The rest should show the courtesy of listening. Now, Raj, you had your hand up."

Raj Patel, who, like Andy, managed a group of project engineers, said, "I agree with Anita. Our environment may create us, but we have a lot of impact on our environment. It depends on how much we want to change. I was born in India, but I made a choice to immigrate to the U.S. in my early twenties. My life, that is, my 'environment,' has been completely different because I made that decision."

"Good point," Jennifer said. "OK. By a show of hands, how many of you feel that your environment creates you?" About a third of the hands went up, but a number of people hesitated to see what Blackburn would do.

"And how many feel you have control over your environment?" Jennifer asked. Again, about a third of the hands went up.

"And how many aren't sure?" she asked. Most of the remaining hands were raised, including Blackburn's.

"So what's the correct answer?" Andy asked. "What's the score here?"

"The correct answer is whatever you believe is correct, Andy," she replied. "But please don't look to me for answers. I'm only the tour guide. You have the answers."

Jennifer continued, "The reason I show this model now is because all learning is about changing our environment in some way or another. The clues of how that is done are partially contained in the upper levels of this pyramid. You will have to wait for that to be revealed later. It's also what this class is about, that is, it's about creating an environment that fits your view of the future. To give you an idea of how we will do this, Jerry will tell us where we will be going today and in the next four days. Jerry?"

Jerry uncovered four wall charts containing the agenda for the four days. It contained a few words but mostly was presented with colorful pictures representing the topics that would be covered. He said that the first two days would be devoted to something called self-cultivation and that it was one hundred percent about each individual in the session. The last two days would be about organizational gardening, which was about creating a culture at Microprojects that would allow the company to excel. He said they might discover, interestingly enough, that self-cultivation was the most important subset of organizational gardening. He pointed to colorful stick figures on the chart sitting on a three-legged stool holding a banner with the word *empowerment* written across it. On each leg was a question mark. He commented that one of the first things the group would do was define empowerment and that it rested on three critical components. If any one of these components was missing, empowerment wouldn't exist, much like the stool would collapse if one of the legs was removed.

Next, he moved on to a picture of a very large tree, which might have represented a redwood. In the ground below the tree, on the roots, were the words *personal power,* which he said was the nutrient that made self-cultivation possible. The next picture was a side view of a large eye with light shining from it. This represented personal vision, and each of them would have the opportunity to determine theirs. Next, he showed the learning pyramid that Jennifer had just introduced, and here too, the four top levels were left blank, but the top level had a picture of the same vision eye. Jerry explained that the learning pyramid reinforced the concept of vision. He next pointed to two large bubbles separated by a two-headed arrow with the word *gap* written above it. In one bubble was written the word *believe,* and in the other the word *do.* He explained this was about something called *our core opportunities.* The next picture was obviously a pea plant. One of the pods was opened, and the seven peas within had the numbers 1 through 7 written on each consecutive pea. He explained that each pea represented a part of the path to significant change and to realizing one's vision. They would discover the significance of each part later.

Jerry moved on to the next chart with the words *organizational gardening* written across the top. He said there were two important parts to organizational gardening: creating the learning organization and leveling the playing field. Pictures of tomato plants gathered in circles with graduation caps and question marks above their heads represented the learning organization, and a huge field of robust corn stalks represented the level playing field. Jerry explained that everyone in the organization would go through the first two days but that the last two days were primarily the responsibility of the management staff, although a portion of it was for everyone.

It took about fifteen minutes to review the agenda, after which he asked if there were any questions. Obviously there were a lot of questions, but everyone sat in a contemplative silence, quizzical expressions on their faces. Jerry waited patiently.

Jennifer reminded the group that Blackburn, in his opening remarks, had said that the program would lay the foundation for a change in culture that would transform the company to an empowered organization. From the corner of the room, Jerry brought out a large three-legged stool with the word *empowerment* written across the seat and question marks drawn on the legs. She said that if they were to empower their workforce, the stability of the stool and the stability of the company rested on the three supporting legs. Each leg represented one of the three components of empowerment. For the next twenty minutes each table would discuss among themselves what they thought these components were.

The discussion became livelier as the time allotted drew to a close. Finally, Jennifer asked each table to share with the entire group what they had decided, starting with table one.

Andy Mills stood and said, "We think the three legs represent sharp, committed people, strong leadership, and competitive compensation".

Anita Hurtado at table two commented, "We feel that the three legs represent knowledge and skills, commitment, and resources". .

Table three and four had something similar. Raj Patel, sitting at table five with Joe Blackburn, said that they thought the three components were knowledge, skills, and clear boundaries.

Jennifer stated, "You've done very well and have come very close". Jerry removed the paper question marks on each leg revealing the words, *how to, want to,* and *OK to.* She continued, "The 'how to' represents the knowledge and skills. The "want to" represents the commitment, motivation, and confidence we need to obtain the "how to". The "OK" to represents the authority we need to act within a given set of boundaries. These components are what the people at Microprojects need to become empowered. The purpose of 'organizational gardening' is to create an environment that makes these components available. Leadership, of course, is also important but mainly in the sense that it helps create the environment, but is not necessarily the environment like in the traditional command and control organization. To put it bluntly, empower people, and then get out of the way".

After a short break, Jerry brought in a large tomato plant containing several large ripe tomatoes. He began by saying, "You will need to use your imagination a little for this part. The concept of the thinking tomato, or 'self-cultivation', is something that a tomato would do if it could think and act on its own. 'Self cultivation' is about taking responsibility and providing your own needs. It is critically necessary because regardless of how hard an organization tries to create the perfect environment, it will invariably miss in some way, shape, or form. Therefore, it behooves all of us to avoid total reliance on the organization to supply our needs by becoming *self leaders*. Of course, the idea of a thinking tomato is only a metaphor because everyone knows tomatoes can't actually think. However, we *can* think and *act,* so we don't have any excuse".

Jerry started laying the foundation for self-cultivation by stating, "Now we are going to do an exercise on personal power. Each of you must list ten ways that you can influence others not counting your present position power".

Andy raised his hand. "What do you mean?" he asked, sounding a little irritated. "If we don't have the positions we have worked for, how can we possibly influence others? The place will turn into a zoo!" A lively discussion at all of the tables ensued. Some of the managers looked very nervous. Blackburn just sat, smiling and saying nothing.

Jennifer interjected, "Please, let me say something. Jerry isn't suggesting that your titles and positions be taken away. He is asking you only to list those things you have going for yourselves that help you influence others to get what you need. It could be knowledge or skills or personal characteristics. I'm sure all of you have a lot more than ten. And, by the way, everyone who can list at least ten will get a prize."

Everyone quieted down and started writing. After about fifteen minutes, Anita Hurtado raised her hand and said, "I have ten."

Jennifer walked over to a box and pulled out a red object about the size of a softball and threw it to Anita. She caught it and after examining it realized it was a round cloth ball filled with beans like a beanbag, and it clearly represented a tomato. Sewn on it were a smiling mouth and two eyes. On the top were two green cloth leaves and, where the stem would be, a cloth exclamation point. Anita seemed very pleased.

This little prize seemed to motivate everyone. Gradually, other participants raised their hands and indicated that they had ten items. Jennifer kept the tomatoes flying.

Just about everyone had a tomato except Mills and Crenshaw, who were still struggling. Jerry asked the rest of the group to help Andy and Jack out.

"Jack and Andy are just being modest," Jerry commented. "Please help them out. Make some observations that'll help them complete their lists."

This was news to everyone. They all knew that modesty was not a trait either one possessed, but they also understood what Jerry was doing. People at Jack and Andy's table and some at an adjacent table made some helpful comments. Finally both raised their hands. Jennifer tossed them their prizes. Andy received his with a smile of relief.

Jerry went through an explanation of personal power and its components, including knowledge, skills, personal characteristics, and, most important, individual relationships with others. He said that sooner or later all of our personal power came down to how we use it to interact with others. He then talked about "the mind doesn't know" adage and the power of seeing one's self in a positive light, and he gave a couple of sports examples to reinforce the idea.

Jennifer said, "This exercise has been about discovering your strengths and positive ways you have to influence others. The foundation of self cultivation is a belief in the self. No matter where you are on the learning continuum, you can use your personal power to reinforce your desire, or "want to," to obtain the knowledge and skills, or "how to," you need. Since you are already in a leadership role, there is another major benefit. Leadership is defined as the ability to influence others, so you can use your personal power to influence people without necessarily having to fall back on the power of your position. Any time that you can lead others without having to remind them that you are the boss, you are ahead. You may at times need your position power, but only as a last resort. You must realize that in an empowered workforce everyone is a leader.

With that they broke for lunch, served in another room. Jennifer and Jerry went to prepare for the afternoon session. A cursory review of the lunch chatter surprisingly indicated that the discussion centered on what had taken place that morning. Everyone seemed engaged and excited about the process. Even Andy and Jack seemed to be coming around.

Chapter Twenty-Four

Understanding "Vision"

While the others were at lunch, Jennifer and Jerry placed large sheets of paper and colored marking pens on the tables. When everyone had returned, Jennifer said, "Most of this afternoon will be devoted to personal vision. We'll have two distinct activities. The first is visualizing what you might be doing in five to ten years. You should think as freely as possible and not impose any limitations. The second activity will be drawing a picture of what you visualized, that is, what is around you, who is there, significant objects that are present, what you are doing, and anything else that is in your mental picture of the future. Please, supply as much relevant detail as possible".

Andy raised his hand—others almost expected this—and said, "But I don't know how to draw."

Jennifer replied, "Artistry is not necessary. Just use stick figures or anything you desire. The important thing is that you first think about who you want to be ten years from now and then use pictures to represent, as much as possible, what you have visualized. Don't worry about the artist part. Your talent may surprise you, Andy. Then you can add that to your personal power list."

This evidently sufficed, because after a period of quiet contemplation, everyone, including Andy, jumped into drawing. The room was completely silent except for the scratching of markers on paper and the sound of classical music in the background. Low-level conversations and laughter could be heard after a half hour or so.

179

When everyone had finished, Jennifer said, "Now each of you in turn are going to share your pictures with the rest of your table."

For the next forty-five minutes they shared their drawings and personal visions with those at their tables. There was a lot of good-natured laughter and commenting, and everyone seemed to take pride in sharing his or her drawing. When they had finished, Jennifer asked if anyone would like to share his or her drawing with the entire class and explain his or her vision of the future.

Anita Hurtato raised her hand and held her picture for everyone to see. The drawing was actually very good. It showed a large house and a car, a woman in a cap and gown, a number of small children sitting in a circle, and a large mountain with a young woman hanging from a ledge. She explained that she had come from a humble background, that her parents were very poor when she was growing up but that they had done everything they could to raise her in a loving environment and see that she acquired an education. She said that the house and car represented financial stability and that these were more for her aging parents who felt that she should have the things they never did. She told the group that the cap and gown represented the PhD she wanted to obtain in economics. She said she had stopped her education after obtaining a BS because she wanted to make money, but she had had a desire for a long time to advance her education. The picture of the mountain represented something she wanted to do because she was afraid of heights. She had always wanted to overcome her fears and climb to new heights in the outdoors. She believed the best way to overcome a fear was to confront it. The last item was the circle of children. She said that she visualized herself having a large family. The best times of her life were when she was with her six brothers and sisters and her parents, so she wanted to create something similar in her life. As she made this comment, Jerry and Jennifer glanced over at each other momentarily. When she sat down, the whole room broke into applause. Anita just smiled, a little embarrassed.

Jennifer said, "Thank you, Anita, for sharing that. My guess is that this isn't the first time you have thought about it." Anita nodded her head in agreement. "I'm surprised that being an artist is not in your picture. Your drawing is good enough for framing." Anita responded that she probably would frame it as a reminder.

"Would anyone else care to share a vision?" Jennifer asked.

Craig Wilson, the purchasing manager, raised his hand and said, "Sure. Why not?" He held up a picture of what appeared to be a large field with a log cabin in the foreground. A large lake was drawn in the background along with snow-capped mountains. A stick figure was fishing, and stick figure deer were roaming in the distance. "Mine's pretty simple. In ten years I plan to be retired. I purchased property in Montana several years ago. I plan to build a log cabin and spend my retirement years hunting and fishing, away from all of the crowds of the Bay Area."

Jennifer said, "Thank you, Craig," as everyone softly applauded. "Anyone else?"

Patel stood and said, "I'll give it a try." He held up a picture of a large house. Standing outside the house were several people. "I mentioned before that I immigrated to the States when I was young. Shortly after arriving here I met my wife, who is also from India, and we were later married. That was twenty years ago. But her aging parents are still there. They visit us every few years, but we have always wanted them to come here and live with us. They have wanted to live here also. I know that will make my wife and our four children tremendously happy. However, it will definitely require a larger house. My drawing is of that house. We've talked about it for years, but, strangely enough, this exercise has made me commit to making it happen." Raj sat down, and the class applauded enthusiastically.

"Anyone else?" Jennifer asked.

Jack Drex, a manager who had been with the company almost since its inception, hesitantly stood and held up his drawing. It seemed to show a man sitting at a desk typing. To the side was a long, thin figure with the word Vietnam written inside. Jack said, "The picture isn't much, but I guess it's what it means to me that's important. Many years ago I served in the war in Vietnam. I say served, but I was drafted; going wasn't my idea at all. It was without a doubt the worst period of my life, but I probably learned more about life and myself in general than at any other time. For years I have wanted to write a book about the experience. I kept a journal the whole time I was there, although now it's tattered, torn and difficult to read in some places. Actually, I had started piecing it all together into a story and have about fifty percent of it written, but I haven't picked it up for years. As I sat here today I kept asking myself 'Why not?' Only people who have experienced war really understand what it is about. It is mankind at its worst. If I can describe my experience, maybe it will help others, show people that war, except in the direst circumstances, is often a futile effort because it results in tremendous destruction and death—death, not of those who started it, but by and large, young innocent people like I was back in the '60s. I saw so many young boys who had their whole lives in front of them die for nothing." Jack stopped for a few moments as if trying to contain his emotions. He concluded, "So thank you, Jennifer and Jerry, for reminding me of this."

Jack must have been very moved by his vision because he had tears in his eyes as he sat down. The whole room was silent. Perhaps they were thinking about what Jack had been through, or maybe they were reliving something from their pasts. No one knew this about Jack; he had never talked about it before. Jerry was thinking about how he really didn't know these people at all; most of his opinions were only surface labels. His general opinion of Blackburn and his staff had been that they were a bunch of pompous asses. But Joe wasn't like that at all. Listening to Joe's staff today, particularly Anita, Raj, and Jack, made him realize how wrong it is to carelessly label people. He needed to make a point of putting this on his core opportunity list.

After a few moments, Jennifer broke the silence and thanked everyone, particularly those who had shared their visions with the class, and said that it was a good time to stop for the day. For homework she asked everyone to think about some things they would like to change in themselves.

Andy Mills raised his hand and asked, "What do you mean?"

Jennifer answered, "If you could take a magic pill and eliminate any bad habits or behaviors, what would those be? Say, something like being short tempered or having a tendency to procrastinate or whatever. Try to come up with at least five."

"I don't think I have five," Andy responded, and several of his peers groaned.

"We'll help you out if you can't think of five," said Hurtado, and everyone laughed.

"We'll talk about this more tomorrow," Jennifer said.

Jerry asked, "How did it go today? Anything we should change? Enough breaks? Anything we could have done differently?"

The consensus was that the day had gone well but they were all exhausted, that this soft stuff could be pretty hard.

Jerry said, "OK, see you tomorrow."

The next day the class began with a centering exercise like on the first day, but this time everyone actively participated. Jerry asked if they had thought about the next four levels of the learning pyramid. He asked each table to discuss what they thought each level was, after which they would open it up to the whole class. Andy asked Jerry to give them a hint. Jerry said the second level had a direct impact on the first level and so on up the pyramid, but the top level had the most impact, although it was only an indirect impact on environment. Lasting change needed the top level. He said the top level had a lot in common with personal vision. Anita said that his hints did more to confuse them than to help them. He said that even so he couldn't help them more. For the next twenty minutes there were lively discussions at each table. Jerry asked for open comments. Raj asked if they should start with level two and work up. Although they didn't get all of the labels exactly right, they came very close and were able to gradually build from environment to behavior to capability to beliefs to identity. Jerry said when we focus on identity, who we want to be, we stand the greatest chance of changing our environment. This model would help them when they looked at the Seven P's, the next subject.

Jerry brought out an object that resembled a large pea pod. He unzipped it and took out seven green balls with the words purpose, passion, process, pace, progress, present, and patience written on individual balls. He gave one of the balls, except patience, to each table and asked them to discuss the meaning. After their discussions, it would be opened up for the whole class to discuss. He said that the Seven P's created the framework to put the journey to their vision in motion. As the whole class discussed each of the P's, Jerry emphasized how it would apply. When they got to process, he used several specific examples to show how it would make it easier to achieve their visions but that there was one process that applied to any vision. This process, called goal setting, allows one to make specific short-term plans to move closer to one's vision. He said goals should follow the SMART acronym; that is, they should be Specific, Motivating, Attainable (but not easy), Relevant, and Trackable. Each spent some time writing specific personal goals.

Jerry demonstrated how communication could often be misleading as he showed the differences between observation and interpretation. He used what he had learned from Mary when she opened his mind to the differences that day, months ago, in her office at the nursery. No one initially showed an understanding; they all came up only with interpretations of Jerry's observable antics. After explaining the difference, he said if they stick to observations when seeking feedback or giving input in situations tinged with emotion, their communication would be much more effective. He passed out a sheet with example statements of observation and interpretation for the class to practice. At the end of the exercise, Blackburn raised his hand and commented that what they had just experienced was perhaps the most single important thing they would learn. Several people raised their hands to ask why. Joe replied that if we all would spend much more time observing and less time interpreting, in time everything else would become self evident.

At the end of the second day, Andy Mills raised his hand. "This has all been a lot of fun, playing these games and drawing and all," he said. "But you are acting like we can create some kind of a miracle. I think you are giving us a lot of false hopes. That's OK for us management types, because most of us are fulfilling our dreams anyway. But if you try to do this stuff with the troops, they're going to end up being frustrated and disappointed. As I said on the first day, we are what we are and nothing much is going to change it."

Jennifer asked, "How many of you feel like Andy?"

A few people raised their hands. Hurtado was shaking her head. Jennifer smiled and walked over to the computer and activated the projector.. She said, "I'm going to show you a picture, and I would like you to discuss at your tables what you see and what kind of person you think this is." She pressed the enter key and displayed a picture of a very large young woman. The woman had a lousy haircut, poor complexion, an unhappy look, and she was dressed like she just pulled her clothes from her closet floor. The discussion brought out comments like "poor self-esteem," "little energy," and "poor health."

Jennifer said, "I'm going to show you an example of the power of vision", as she pressed the enter key again. "This is the same woman today," she said as the projector flashed a picture of herself on the screen. "Never underestimate the power of vision," she added. The whole room sat in complete stunned silence. Andy's hand dropped down to his bulging belly. "See you tomorrow," Jennifer said, turning off the projector.

When everyone had left, Jerry turned to Jennifer and said, "Well, that was quite a surprise. I think you may have even swayed Andy. You certainly shut him up. Showing those pictures took a lot of courage, Jennifer."

"Oh, I don't think so," she responded, smiling. "The only concern I had was that some of them might have thought I was bragging, and that wasn't my intent at all. I think it is important to share something personal, something that changes the 'vision thing' from possibility to probability and then reality. If just one of them embraces the power of vision, it was worth it. Sometimes making it personal is the best way to teach a concept."

As Jerry and Jennifer were leaving, they ran into Blackburn, although it looked like he may have been waiting for them. "Great job today, guys," he said, smiling and slowly nodding.

"Thanks, Joe," both replied.

Joe seemed a little uneasy, like he wanted to say something but wasn't sure he should, which wasn't like him at all. Jennifer and Jerry were starting to feel a little uncomfortable when Joe said, "I thought this stuff on 'self-cultivation' and the Seven P's would have an impact on the company, but I didn't realize it would have such an impact on me. The one that really grabbed me, though, was the one about every occasion being an opportunity for learning, about focusing on the learning value rather than all of the sorrow and regrets."

Joe looked off in the distance as if considering how to express his thoughts. Jerry and Jennifer were wondering what to say when Joe continued. "It made me recall my whole career at Microprojects. I feel my work life has been exceptional. I have enjoyed my time there tremendously. Now, Jim Crabtree and the board are considering me for CEO. I guess that means I have been successful," he said and stared off again at the waves breaking against the rugged cliff in the distance.

After another awkward silence, he continued, "While I've been a resounding success in the business world, I have been an abject failure in my personal life. My ten-year marriage to my childhood sweetheart, Susan, ended in a divorce seventeen years ago. They say there are always two sides to a story when a marriage dissolves, but in our case most of the fault was mine. I had no problem spending sixteen-hour days, and sometimes longer, working, but I could rarely take just a few hours to be with her. And my social activities were always centered on work. For several years after we were married, Susan would tag along. At some point she must have gotten bored with the whole thing, but I was too blind to see. I thought she should revel in my glory. Strange that I should think that! One reason I liked her was because she was so independent-minded.

"I was in love with her when we got married, I was in love with her when we parted, and I still love her today. But it's too late because she's remarried and has a child. She always wanted to have children, but I thought kids would interfere with my career. I've learned three things over the last couple of days. First, that I was to blame for the failure of my marriage. Second, that it's time to move on because I will never be able to repair the damage I did. And third, and most important, if I am ever so fortunate as to have a relationship with someone like Susan again, that will be the most important thing in my life.

"That's what part of my vision of the future looks like, guys. I need to shed some of my responsibilities, which shouldn't be such a problem when our new culture is in place. So I hope this stuff works," he said, smiling. "I think it all really crystallized when Jennifer showed her photo today. You may have grabbed a lot of people by the gut; you certainly did me. So, thanks, guys, for a great day and thanks for listening to an old man ramble on. This session is exceeding my expectations, and I look forward to the next two days." He grasped their hands in his and squeezed them and smiled. "See you tomorrow," he said as he walked off.

Jennifer and Jerry stared at each other for a moment, and Jennifer said, "I'm sure that wasn't easy, but he seemed relieved to have shared it with someone," as she watched Joe depart. "He's quite a man," she added, smiling.

Jerry just said, "Yeah. Of course, he wasn't at our site when he and his wife divorced. We had only heard that he was married before, but there were no details, even with the amount of gossip that goes on at Microprojects. His last comment is good advice for us all and, strangely enough, it's very similar to what Mary learned from her tragedy."

The next two days went very well. Using various games and exercises and the ever-present music, Jennifer and Jerry led the group through the discovery of the power of open communication, empathic listening, and the true meaning of generative learning. There was a lot of dialogue about the incentive systems they had used over the years. A special team was picked to look at alternative incentive systems that would create a level playing field for all employees and motivate the entire workforce. The highlight of the session may have been when Jennifer had the whole group dancing the Jewish wedding dance. Jerry knew the session was a success when he saw the great "player of no games" Mills adding some special twists and moves to the dance. Jennifer and Jerry were warmly applauded at the end of the session, and the group unanimously decided the program should be rolled out to all employees.

Jennifer and Jerry celebrated at the same French restaurant in Carmel that Friday night. As they toasted the success with champagne, Jerry said, "You were great, Jennifer. I learned a lot from you this week."

"You weren't so bad yourself, Jerry," Jennifer responded. "This facilitation stuff seems to come natural to you."

"I think the self-cultivation I have been doing had a lot to do with it. Six months ago I don't believe I would have been able to stand up in front of a group of people and do something like this. Now I can hardly wait for the next session. And without what we learned in Gail's accelerated learning class, it would have been a lot more difficult. It's one thing to have a message, which we do have, but delivering it so that people comprehend, and, most important, commit to practicing it, is a whole different challenge. I have never had as much fun at work. I almost feel guilty accepting pay for it!"

"I know what you mean, Jerry. I feel the same, but I need to question the 'almost feel guilty' part. I think we earned our pay this week. I am mentally and physically drained."

"Me too. I think we make a pretty good team. Doing it alone wouldn't have been nearly as much fun."

"I agree," said Jennifer.

"You . . . you know, Jennifer," Jerry said, stammering a bit. "I've never shared with you my vision. I have been thinking about it a lot lately."

"Visions are like that," Jennifer said, smiling warmly. "Would you like to share it now?"

"Well, uh . . . that is, you see . . . Jennifer, you are part of it," Jerry said as he twisted the linen napkin around his hand.

"I am?" Jennifer asked with a bright smile. "In what way?"

"Yes," Jerry said. "I see myself doing work like we did this past week; helping companies be happier, more-productive places for their people, and helping people see the freedom that comes with personal responsibility and self-cultivation. And I don't necessarily see myself just doing that at Microprojects either, Jennifer. I would like to start my own consulting firm and work with all sorts of companies."

"And you want me to work with you?" Jennifer asked anxiously.

"Well, I, uh, I, you see, I . . . My vision has more to it than that. I was, that is, I was thinking that I want you to be more than a business partner. I want you to be my partner for life. I want you to be my wife, Jennifer. I want to share the rest of my life with you."

Tears came to Jennifer's eyes as she reached across the table and grabbed his hands. People at the surrounding tables started looking at them. "Yes, Jerry," Jennifer said quietly, savoring the moment. "No offer could ever make me happier!"

Chapter Twenty-Five

Wonders and Weddings

A couple of weeks after the pilot session, Jerry and Jennifer were in Jerry's office talking when Gene Larson stuck his head in and said, "Hey guys, congratulations! I just received the letter announcing your engagement. Everyone's talking about it; must be going to be a big affair. Are you inviting the whole site?"

"Well, not everyone, but almost," Jerry replied. "Mary Green has offered to host the wedding at her place. We're probably going to set the date for the middle of September."

"I can hardly wait," said Gene. "Hey, by the way, what did you two do to Mad Man Mills?"

"What do you mean?" Jerry asked.

"Well, first of all, last evening I was driving to the store and I see Mills out jogging! Did you hear me? Mills? Jogging? Can you imagine carrying that gut along at a twelve-minute mile pace? Got the fancy new shoes and bright gaudy running outfit to boot; it was sure a sight to see. Then the next day I'm in my office when he calls and asks if I he can stop by. Can you believe Mills asking anyone below him if he can stop by? I thought this must be some serious stuff if he was asking if he could stop by. I figured I was probably going to be fired, but I couldn't think of anything I had done wrong lately. So Mills comes in, closes the door, and I think, 'Oh no.' But he proceeded to tell me what a good job I'd been doing and apologized for not being more supportive. I thought, *What does this guy want?* and I was ready to do anything as long as he didn't ask me to go jogging with him. But he didn't want anything. He just said I could expect a new leadership style from him and that I should make sure I attend your class. Can you imagine that? I was dumbfounded. I couldn't think of a thing to say!"

"*You* couldn't think of anything to say? Well, stranger things have happened," Jerry replied.

"I can't imagine where," Gene said as he walked out of the office, shaking his head. "I can't imagine where."

September rolled around, and the Bay Area weather changed from fog on the coast and almost unbearable heat inland to a typical Indian summer—perfect temperatures from the coast to the Sierras. More often than not, September, October, and sometimes November are the best months of the year in the Bay Area. Many a tourist with shorts and a light shirt has been unpleasantly surprised by the cold foggy weather in the city and along the northern coast of California in the supposedly hot summer months of July and August.

The weather in the Bay Area was not all that was changing. Things were starting to show a discernible difference at Microprojects. Jerry and Jennifer had conducted almost thirty sessions with a cross section of people, and although they had not yet hit critical mass, the mood and the attitude were on a definite, positive upward swing. In addition to the sessions on organizational gardening and self-cultivation, employees were enthusiastically attending classes that would help them in their particular fields. The "bottom line" was that Microprojects' profits were in the black for the first time in several quarters, and its stock was starting to climb at a very satisfactory rate for the stockholders. Crabtree had stepped down as CEO and passed the baton to Blackburn. Joe had asked Jennifer and Jerry to work on a plan for introducing the program at Microprojects' sister plants in Austin and Atlanta.

On a smaller scale, Jerry's garden had almost become a consistent source of produce for the neighbors. The tomatoes and other vegetables grew so profusely that he had had a hard time getting rid of them, much less eating all of them himself.

Jennifer and Jerry were making last-minute preparations for their wedding the coming weekend. Jennifer's two brothers and Jerry's two brothers were flying in from back east with Jerry's mother. A total of three hundred people were coming. The Green Patch nursery was scheduled to be closed so all could attend.

The day of the wedding arrived, and the weather, as predicted, was another perfect day. The wedding took place outside. Mary had decorated the grounds to reflect the festive occasion. Jennifer's oldest brother accompanied her down the bridal path, and Jerry's mother stood with him at the makeshift altar. Vows exchanged and wet eyes dried, the champagne was opened and the band began playing. Jerry and Jennifer circulated to say hello to their guests and to thank them for coming. They were looking for Mary, whom they hadn't seen for a while, to thank her for everything she had done. As they slowly wove through the crowd, they spotted Natalie talking to, of all people, Gene Larson. Natalie was almost in tears, laughing at something Gene had said.

After hugs and congratulations, Jerry asked, "Have either of you seen Mary? We've been looking all over for her and can't find her anywhere."

Natalie responded, "Actually, I did see her over by the rose garden talking to Blackburn."

"With Blackburn? Now that's interesting," said Jerry.

"What have you got there, Jer?" asked Gene. "Something for the grapevine?"

"I just said that it was interesting, Gene. You'll have to fill in the blanks yourself," said Jerry.

"Well, someone has to keep the 'vine going since you became part of management," Gene said. "By the way, I saw Mills dancing with Marie Evans a while ago; at least I think he meant it to look like dancing. It looked like he was jogging to music. I'll plant a few of those tidbits in the organizational soil on Monday. But I have to give him credit: he *has* taken several inches off his waist, and it's been a pleasure working for him since he's been 'tomatoized'."

"Tomatoized?" asked Jennifer.

"That's Gene's word for what we have been teaching people at our sessions, Jennifer," said Jerry.

"I thought about calling it 'tomato-ated,' but 'ized' seemed to be more fitting. Otherwise people might get confused and think it's

about eating something. 'Ya eat da tomato and it transforms ya,"
Gene clowned. "And speaking of eating something, I think I'll go
get some more food *and* something else to drink. A couple of more
glasses of champagne, and I may challenge Mills to a dance-a-thon,"
Gene said as he grabbed Natalie by the hand and walked off toward
the buffet. Natalie glanced back with a puzzled look on her face but
seemed to be enjoying Gene and his humor.

Jennifer and Jerry, after working through the crowd and the
congratulations, finally found Mary and Joe sitting on a bench by the
rose garden. Both seemed to be in intense conversation as Jennifer
and Jerry walked up without being seen. This wasn't surprising
since Joe and Mary, true to form, were usually totally absorbed in
whatever they were doing.

"I see the two of you have met," Jerry said.

"Well if it isn't the newlyweds," Mary said as she stood up and
embraced Jennifer and Jerry. "I'm so happy for you," she said with
tears in her eyes. "Actually, this isn't the first time we met. Joe, it
seems, is an orchid lover. He was in the nursery some time back,"
she said, looking at Joe slyly.

Joe added his congratulations and hugged them. "The encounter
she's referring to was very brief. At last I get to really meet the lady
you have told me so much about, Jerry," Joe said, looking over at
Mary with obvious delight. "We were just talking about your favorite
subject, guys. I'm trying to convince Mary to come and work for us,
but I think she may be swaying me to quit Microprojects and go
work for her. Says she needs someone in the orchid department," he
said with a laugh.

"Mary, we want to thank you for everything you have done for
us. Of all the people in the world, what has happened to us would
not have been possible without you," said Jennifer. "Taking me in
when I was an overweight ball of self-pity, teaching me, and us, all
you have. Just the word *thanks* seems so small compared to what we
have received."

"I feel the same way," said Jerry. "I still remember that day I
walked into your nursery, totally dejected; you transformed my life.
And Joe, the faith and trust and the opportunities you have given me
. . . I am tremendously indebted."

"You both have repaid me many times over," Joe said as Mary nodded in agreement. "But it all goes back to this lady here," Joe said, looking over at Mary admiringly.

"And you the great orchid grower," she said, looking at Joe. She continued. "We've never talked about this, but it's really about something called *acting on the brief moment of chance.* There are so many unexplainable things that happen in our life. The only thing that *can* explain them is that they are due to chance, to random occurrences. Things happen. They are more obvious when we examine our past, the supposedly small, insignificant things that took place, but if they hadn't happened, our lives would have taken a completely different direction. It's really a coincidence, but Joe and I were just talking about this. Take for instance the way I met John; I needed another class and off-handedly decided to take a class in physics to complete my schedule. It was on nothing but a whim. John was a good lookingTA helping teach one of the labs, and that was how we met. Totally chance, like the day you walked into the nursery feeling like your life was a waste, or the way that Natalie decided to come to work for The Green Patch, bringing with her the basis for the management philosophy we have adopted, which is now the basis for the cultural changes at Microprojects. It's all pretty much random, but the thinking tomato learns to recognize these moments and act on them. Who knows what spin-offs of fortune will occur just because the two of you were married today? Things that people may look back on years from now and say, 'You know, if we hadn't gone to Jennifer and Jerry's wedding, such and such wouldn't have happened.' " She and Joe looked at each other and smiled.

Jennifer said, "What you say is very interesting Mary. I never planned to work for a nursery. One day I was looking at the want ads in the paper and I ran across your nursery ad. I checked it out on, as you say, a whim. Now look at the tremendous change it has brought about in my life."

"We're glad we found the two of you together. We have some news for you. A dream of mine, or should I say *ours,* " Jerry said, grasping Jennifer's hand, "is to have our own consulting company, to help other organizations realize what has, or is, happening at Microprojects, to share with others what you and Joe and others have taught us. We've decided to start a company. We're going to call it The Thinking Tomato, and the basis of our teachings will be the Seven P's.

"While that means we'll no longer be your employees, we want you both to know that it has nothing to do with either of you. Working with both of you has been the most exciting experience for us," said Jennifer. "We just want to spread out and be on our own. And if things work out right, we plan to contribute at least twenty percent of our time *pro bono* in the high schools where this learning is desperately needed and with other nonprofits."

Mary and Joe stood there in silence until Joe said, "Well, double congratulations are in order. I'm sure Mary will join me in wishing you success. But I hope you'll tie up the loose ends at work before you leave."

"Absolutely," Jerry said. "We don't really plan to go anywhere. We'll be around. We both love the Bay Area and are thinking about moving a little south of here to the Santa Cruz or Capitola area. We wouldn't leave it half done, Joe. We've made a commitment to you and Microprojects."

"I know you wouldn't, guys," said Joe.

"You two better get back to your guests," said Mary. "Besides, Joe and I have some things to talk about concerning purchasing a new computer system to modernize the nursery. He promised to give me a good price."

As Jennifer and Jerry walked back to where the guests were eating, drinking, and dancing, Jennifer looked at Jerry and said, "I think they just wanted to be alone. What do you think?"

"Yeah. Wouldn't that be something if the two of them got together? You talk about a powerhouse of brainpower. Shoot, maybe they're getting ready to grab on to that brief moment of chance," he said as he smiled at Jennifer. "Wonders never cease, and stranger things have happened." They both looked over to watch Andy Mills and Gene Larson trying to outdo each other with their dance moves.

And those tomato plants just kept on growing, but no one knew *what* they were really thinking.

The End

(and the beginning)